EZANA
AND THE
LOVEBIRD

A CALL TO LEGENDARY ADVENTURES

BERHANE NEGUSSIE

Cover Design: REBECACOVERS
Interior Design: Jennie Lyne Hiott
Editor: Meagan Thompson
Distribution: HIDRINA

Printed in Canada
First Printing, 2021
ISBN 978-1-7774171-0-9

Berhane Negussie
Brinnium@gmail.com

For Seble, Alula, and Saba

1

I KNOW WHAT EZANA DID LAST SUMMER

For one super reason, Ezana disliked going back to school at the end of each summer. He hated the question, "How did you spend your summer?" each teacher asked on the first day of the school—sometimes the whole first week of school.

Ezana's hard-working parents sent him to one of the best schools in the neighborhood. Most of his classmates had the opportunity to go to cool places for their summer vacations. Ezana, on the other hand, didn't go anywhere but read the comic books he loved and watch superhero movies he adored so much on *Netflix*.

His mom and his dad took him to some community activities in Denver. Still, Ezana didn't dare to talk about those activities in front of the super-rich kids who visited awesome places like Disneyland, Niagra Falls, Universal Studios, Paris, Rome, Edinburgh, Tokyo, and Dubai during their school breaks. That's why he hated going to school after summer break.

In recent years, his classmates started to pay special attention to him. When Ezana said, "I didn't go anywhere," most of the students exploded in laughter, except Grace, who always showed him sympathy.

Ezana's mom, Tsehay, and his dad, Yared, were excellent parents, but they were busy in their 7-Eleven store business. Financially, Tsehay and Yared supported their extended families back home in Tigray.

And the entire class would laugh at him. To avoid such embarrassing moments, Ezana pretended to be sick and skipped classes at the beginning of each school year.

After skipping class the first week, Ezana walked into class one Monday morning. When the teacher started the lesson of the day, a boy raised his hand and intervened.

"What's up, Oliver?" the teacher asked.

"Ezana was absent and didn't get the chance to talk about his summer vacation," Oliver said as innocent as possible.

Ezana jolted and sweat started rolling inside his school uniform instantly.

Grace saw when Oliver smirked to his friends, and they gave him the thumbs-up sign.

"Class, do you want to hear Ezana's story?" the teacher asked.

"Yes, sir!" students shouted excitedly.

Grace gazed across at Ezana. His hands trembled and sweat broke out all over his body. *I gotta do something,* Grace said to herself.

The teacher put his learning materials back on a table on his side of the room. "Okay, Ezana, come up here and tell us what you did last summer!" the teacher exclaimed.

Suddenly, a scream exploded, and something dropped on the floor. Everyone in the class jarred and stood to look at what happened. That was Grace who collapsed on the floor. Ezana ran toward her, but the teacher arrived before him and lifted her up.

"Open the door for me," the teacher shouted and rushed to take her to the school clinic.

On her way out, while on the teacher's arms, Grace winked at Ezana with a faint smile. He stopped dead in his tracks and didn't follow after her to the clinic. Grace went the extra mile to save him, and that extreme kindness touched Ezana's heart. That's when he decided it was time to go somewhere amazing and worth talking about during the first week of the school.

birthday. He fancied visiting a landmark, at least for his cool friend, Grace, who always rooted and fought for him.

In the evening of the day Grace saved him at school, Ezana heard his parents arriving home from work and walked down from his bedroom to the living room.

"Dad, Mom, I want to go to Disneyland for my twelfth birthday!" Ezana shouted without saying hello.

"Baby, you have ten months until your next birthday," his mom, Tsehay, said a little tired of talking about his birthday all the time.

"And how about a kiss first?" She stopped and waited for him to kiss her. He kissed her and looked around for his dad, Yared.

"Where is Dad?" Ezana asked.

"He is in the basement," she said and went to the refrigerator to store the food she brought in.

Ezana walked down the stairs to the basement to hug his dad, and they came back to the living room together.

"Did your dad hear what you said?" Tsehay asked sarcastically.

"Hear what?" Yared asked.

"It is the first week of September, and he is talking about his birthday in July," she said, still working in the refrigerator.

"I want to go to Disneyland on this one. I'm warning you early so that you can make plans ahead of time. Otherwise, I'll join Grace's family on their summer vacation to anywhere," Ezana said with authority in his voice.

"I've never heard of such a tone before," Yared said, sitting on the couch and reaching for the TV remote control at the same time.

"Maybe it's a new tone because a new event happened at school today."

Yared turned off the TV. Tsehay stopped storing food in the refrigerator and joined her husband on the couch to hear what happened. Ezana explained to them not only what happened that day but also in the previous years. He narrated the story as dramatic and as moving as possible that forced tears of care to roll down on Tsehay's face. Yared embraced and squeezed her hard.

It was that night in the bedroom that his parents secretly planned a surprise trip. Even though Ezana kept asking and reminding them about it, they only told him that they designed a pleasant surprise for his birthday.

3

THE UNPLEASANT BIRTHDAY SURPRISE

I n mid-July 2016, when it was a week away from his birthday, Ezana, Tsehay, and Yared checked in at Denver International Airport. Ezana was so excited when he knew that their flight was to Los Angeles, California, because all his favorite fun places were located in California, including Disneyland, Universal Studios, and Sea World.

When they landed in Los Angeles's LAX airport, his dad approached him and said, "We are not there yet. Our final destination is not here. We'll be connecting to another flight."

"What?" Ezana looked up at his dad and started walking fast, pulling his carry on behind him.

"We said it's a surprise, remember?" yelled Tsehay from behind.

"This is such an unpleasant surprise," Ezana cried, walking away from them.

While waiting to connect flight, Ezana sat alone among stranger passengers. He wished his parents left him behind in Denver with one of his cousins like they did before. He walked to the enormous glassed window of the airport and stared at the tall buildings of downtown Los Angeles. An idea hit him right there. He unzipped his carry-on luggage and checked the money he saved over the year.

"I'm not going back to school without any story worth telling. Never again," he promised himself. "I have to run away from here for a couple

of days on our way back home. It would be a more interesting story to tell in the class." The idea made him feel better and cheered him up.

"See you soon for an adventure LA," Ezana said.

The boarding gate for Northern Star Airlines opened, and the staff started boarding passengers by zones. The Denver family connected their flight to Mekelle, Tigray.

4

SWEETER THAN HONEY

zana rubbed his eyes a million times and complained about his
itching eyes, tired of watching the screen, and he slept the entire
flight. Tsehay and Yared, on the other hand, were excited to go
back to their birthplaces. They were thrilled to see their family and
friends. Their last trip to Tigray was only two years ago, but it was
sorrowful and short. Tsehay and Yared made that unfortunate trip after
Tsehay lost her father in a car accident. They flew without Ezana for a
few days to attend the funeral, and it was a terrible trip to remember.

Tsehay and Yared glowed in excitement when the plane touched
down at Mekelle's Alula Aba Nega International airport. Ezana, not
only exhausted but also unhappy about the destination of the trip,
lagged behind when they walked to the airport carousel. Tsehay and
Yared used Ezana's slowness as an excuse to take some pictures on the
runway.

They fetched their luggage from the carousel and went straight to
Aksum Hotel where they had booked their room online weeks earlier.
After they slept off the jet lag and fatigue, Ezana's parents took him to
meet his grandmother on his mother's side.

Ezana smiled for the first time since LAX airport. His grandma
cheered him up in the way she welcomed them home. He had seen
when women said, "Elelelelele" to express their joy before, but the way
his grandma did it was exceptional and lovely.

Before they moved back to Tigray for good, Tsehay's mom and dad used to live in Denver. Ezana's grandma babysat him until he was three. She was elated to see her grandson all grownup.

He enjoyed the breakfast she served to them—two kinds of local bread, Himbasha and Hibishti, with white honey, juice, and tea. His dad told him that it was the continental breakfast of the Tigray people.

Ezana liked everything about his grandma. The way she talked and called everyone had a uniqueness and sweetness to it. The Tigrigna word "mearey" was her favorite name, which she used to call everyone. Mearey meant "honey," but her mearey felt sweeter than honey itself. Everything she said and everything she did attracted him. Cooking and feeding the family was her ideal job. She was the sweetest, and he loved her instantly. Later that day, Ezana revealed his admiration for his grandmother to his mom, which made Tsehay's face sparkle.

"Your grandma credits her charm for her Raya and Enderta mixed heritage," Tsehay explained.

Ezana made a mental note to Google later that night about the history and cultures of the Raya and Enderta people of Tigray, as he always did when he heard new information.

"And that charming grandma raised you with love and care," Yared reminded Ezana.

"She is sweeter than the honey she served us," Ezana said.

5

CALL TO ADVENTURE: FROM MUSEE PICASSO TO ART PALACE

Ezana did not crack a smile since he learned their final destination wasn't California. He didn't care where they went next. Through the long flight from Los Angeles to Mekelle, he killed many hours watching several superhero movies and sleeping. He was exhausted by the long trip from Denver to Los Angeles to Mekelle and got moody when they checked into a hotel for a couple of days.

"This is the most unpleasant surprise of all time," he kept complaining.

Still, Ezana didn't get his dad's attention. Yared was busy planning a little surprise to please his wife. Anyone who wanted to surprise Tsehay needed one keyword: artwork.

When Tsehay went down to the hotel lobby, Yared told his plan to Ezana and asked him to join him in surprising her. But Ezana was still mad at them and preferred to stay in the hotel, read his comic books, play games or watch movies.

"I thought it was my birthday, not Mom's," he complained.

"Do you want to see your mom happy or not? Besides, you love art too. Don't you?" Yared asked and didn't wait for Ezana's answer. "Let's go for quick walk."

Father and son went out for a quick walk in the streets of Mekelle. While walking, Yared told Ezana the story of how his mom became a die-hard art lover.

"When Tsehay was in college, one of her professors gave her the assignment to read about Pablo Escobar and do a presentation in class. She went to a library and asked a librarian to give her books on Pablo. The librarian gave her books written about Pablo Picasso, not Pablo Escobar, but she didn't notice the difference." Yared paused to measure Ezana's interest.

"Oh, poor Mom!" Ezana said, amazedly.

Yared beamed when Ezana got hooked and continued narrating the story.

"Tsehay read the books and was blown away by Pablo Picasso's great works and eccentric character. One book led to another, and she fell in love with the extraordinary artist who was one of the greatest and most influential artists of the 20th century. The professor excused her for mistaking Pablo Escobar for Pablo Picasso and allowed her to do the presentation anyway.

"Soon, she became an aesthete, a person who loves and appreciates artwork, and she made friends with similar passions. Tsehay liked to refer to her stumbling at the library as The Call to Adventure." Yared paused again.

"This is interesting trivia, Dad. How come you guys didn't tell me before?" Ezana questioned.

"Wait, there is more," Yared said and continued. "One of Tsehay's college friends, an international student from France, hosted her in Paris one summer. Both huge Pablo Picasso fans, they wanted to see at least five thousand out of the fifty thousand artworks he did. They started at Mussee Picasso in Paris and traveled to Barcelona and Malaga, Spain. They visited the two most famous Picasso museums and his birthplace. Thousands of Picasso artworks later, the girls got back in Paris and went to see Leonardo da Vinci's masterpiece, the Mona Lisa at Musee du Louvre.

"After that epic trip, Tsehay became known for her love of artwork both in college and in her community. On graduation day, her Tigrayan friend gave her a unique art called 'Sacred Landscapes of Tigray.' The beautiful art opened another window to the elegant church artworks of Tigray.

"The one hanging in our living room?" Ezana asked.

"That's right," Yared said.

"She also became a big fan of the famous artist Desta Hagos after she bought her avant-garde artwork online."

"Another one hanging in our living room?" Ezana asked.

"Right again," Yared replied. "Later, Tsehay found out Desta Hagos, the first female artist to hold a solo art exhibition in Ethiopian history, was opening a show in Thousand Oaks, California. She called in sick to work and flew to California to attend the art exhibition. Tsehay enjoyed Desta's magnificent artworks presented in the California Lutheran University, from where the artist graduated. And to Tsehay's surprise, she had the chance to meet and had coffee with the charming and down to earth artist."

"This explains everything about the art lover, Mom," Ezana said.

"And it also explains who influenced you to love art too," Yared said.

"Awesome. Let's do it, Dad. Let's surprise Mom," Ezana said.

***

Yared knew art was the easy way to please his wife and put a smile on his son's face. He wanted their stay in Mekelle to be memorable and arranged everything with the help of his resourceful friend who lived in the city.

Yared's friend picked them up from the hotel and drove them via Hawelti to Adi Hawsi. Ezana looked at the city he never knew before. From Yared's excitement, Tsehay knew something was going on, but she didn't ask.

Yared's friend parked his car in front of a two-story building and said, "Welcome to Tigray in Canvas, also known as the Palace of Art."

"Yessss!" Tsehay screamed.

A curator was waiting for them inside the compound. He described the philosophy behind the architecture of the building and the visionary who built and dedicated it to Tigrayan art and artists.

"This is genius! Who's the visionary, the genius behind this incredible idea?" Tsehay asked.

"You will find out at the end," the curator replied.

It was built recently, and Tsehay didn't know such a wonderful place existed. She listened to the curator with all ears. Ezana looked fascinated too, which made Yared more elated.

While everybody was in awe, the curator took them to the studio/ gallery and allowed them to take a moment to see all the incredible pieces of artwork. Quietly, three of them scanned the depiction of Tigray's modern, medieval and ancient history, culture, and nature.

"This face looks very familiar?" Tsehay said after her eyes landed on a graceful man's portrait.

"That's Prince Mengesha Seyoum," Yared snapped.

"And the visionary behind this Palace of Art," the curator added.

"Oh! Now it makes a lot of sense," Tsehay said, and Yared nodded in agreement.

"As you can see, it's designed to serve as a residence, studio, and gallery for aspiring artists. The architectural design of the entire building also reflects the Palace of Emperor Yohannes IV. The prince's homage to his great grandfather.

The whole building could be turned into an exhibition and can showcase two hundred artworks. Every piece of material used for the building was intended to correlate with Tigray's nature, culture, and history. Anything applied has a purpose for inspiration and aesthetic," the curator said.

"Job well done! It's literally Tigray in Canvas and a luxurious feast for the soul," Tsehay whispered.

Yared agreed and nodded.

Ezana didn't hear what they were saying because his attention was captivated by a particular painting for a reason he didn't understand. He tried to look at all the artworks evenly, but he kept going back to that piece.

Curious, Ezana started asking the curator thousands of questions about the artworks. The curator appreciated his interest and gave him a special tour around the prince's paint house and showed him some of the prince's private art collections. Then, to Ezana's surprise, he saw the same painting grabbed his attention again in the prince's private room.

On their way out from the prince's room, Ezana stayed behind, and he looked at the painting at close range. He tried to analyze the uniqueness of the art and involuntarily touched it. Then his entire body lit up from an electrical shock. He was too startled to move and stood there frozen.

"What was that?" Ezana shouted.

"Are you okay, young man?" the curator asked as he came back for Ezana.

"I'm all right," Ezana said, waking up from his shock.

"This must be the most under-appreciated, under-visited, and under-publicized art museums in the world," Tsehay said to herself.

After an incredible time at Tigray in Canvas, coffee at Enda Ra'esi, the former residence of Prince Mengesha Seyoum, worked out perfectly.

6

SASHIMI OF LAKE HASHENGE

Tsehay's uncle, Yohannes, whom she liked to call Uncle John, wanted to take her and her family for lunch. He was on field work somewhere out of Mekelle and arranged a lunch date over the phone with her. Tsehay reminded Yared and Ezana a million times about the lunch date. She also told them how her uncle was a funny, spontaneous, and likable person. The information she poured over them made even Ezana interested to meet the guy.

They all waited for him in the garden of the hotel. Yohannes arrived on time. He passionately hugged and kissed all three of them, and looked and sounded thrilled to meet them.

Ezana's original plan was just to meet the guy to make his mom happy and then stay in the hotel room, but surprisingly, Ezana preferred to have lunch with them.

"What do you guys want to eat?" Yohannes asked.

"Anything," Yared said.

Tsehay nodded to agree with her husband.

"You guys are too old to speak your minds. What do you like to eat, King Ezana?" Yohannes asked Ezana.

Ezana liked Yohannes even more for addressing him as a king after his namesake. His parents looked at him as if to convince him to agree with them. Ezana hesitated.

"Come on. Don't be shy. Tell me anything you like," Yohannes encouraged Ezana.

"Anything?" Ezana asked.

"Anything for the king," Yohannes replied.

"How about sushi?" Ezana said.

"Baby, I don't think there is a sushi restaurant here," Tsehay said.

Both Yared and Yohannes nodded to agree with her.

"But the king wants sushi for lunch. You can't say no to a king."

Yohannes pulled his phone out and excused himself to make a quick phone call.

Tsehay and Yared were so thrilled Ezana decided to join them for lunch that they didn't complain about his fancy idea. Yohannes came back with a plan and led them to his double cab car.

"To fulfill King Ezana's special request, I'm going to do something crazy. May I get the king's blessing?" Yohannes asked Ezana.

"One hundred percent," Ezana said, laughing.

"Va bene! Buckle up. We are in for a long ride."

"If you tell us what you did in Rome, we will go wherever you take us," Tsehay said.

Yohannes nodded and hit the gas pedal.

7

ROMANCE IN ROME AND THE RUNAWAY GROOM

Yohannes, also known as John, received his education of archeology at the American University of Rome, Italy. While he was in high school, he developed an interest in archeology, and he searched for universities that granted a degree in archeology. Yohannes targeted Italian universities since his favorite aunt was in Milan. The American University of Rome became his first choice because they taught in English.

When he asked his aunt to help, she agreed to sponsor him if his parents allowed him to go abroad. His patriotic and conservative parents accepted the idea on the condition that he should come back home and serve his people. Yohannes agreed. He loved his country and the people, especially ancient history and civilization. That was why he chose to study archeology.

When Yohannes got to Rome, he fell in love at first sight. He loved both the past and present dimensions of the city. The archeological, historical sites, and museums of Rome inspired him. He felt proud of himself for choosing to become an archeologist.

Back home, Yohannes used to hear that French was the most romantic, but Italian sounded the most poetic to his ears. Gelato also became his weakness quickly.

When class started at the American University of Rome, Yohannes realized his afro hair and short stubble got him the attention of beautiful girls, which made him a little uncomfortable and shy.

To stay away from the charming beauties of the city, he started a hobby of going to the Dogali Obelisk located near the Termini of Roma. The moment Yohannes found the obelisk, he felt as happy as a duck getting in the water for the first time. He didn't know about the existence of the statue and the square Piazza dei Cinquecento, which were built and named in memory of the Italian army defeated by Alula, the right hand of Emperor Yohannes IV of Ethiopia, in the battle of Dogali. Yohannes was given the name after Emperor Yohannes IV and raised by victorious stories, and for him to discover that statue in the heart of Rome was a miracle. Every weekend, trips to the Dogali Obelisk with a book helped him stay connected with his roots during the entire degree program at the university.

While enjoying Rome without losing his purpose, one Sunday afternoon, Yohannes noticed a gorgeous Italian girl passing by. He felt like he was hit by thunder for sitting too much under the Dogali Obelisk. He couldn't stop thinking about her the whole week. Usually, he read a book on a train from the university to Termini, and he continued reading while sitting on the steps under the obelisk. But after he saw the beautiful girl, he couldn't focus. Instead, he folded the book and waited to see her passing by.

He didn't stop there. He became curious about where she went every week at the same time, and one day, he followed her. After a ten minutes' walk from the Dogali Obelisk, she walked into an ice cream shop, The Gelatist. Following her back and forth became his secret addiction for a few weeks.

The pretty girl from Rome wasn't stupid. She noticed he was following her to and from the ice cream shop, and he was getting closer to her day by day. One day, right before she entered the ice cream parlor, she turned around and faced him.

"Ciao, are you following me?"

"Yes. It's been weeks since I followed you, and you should pay me," Yohannes replied unflinchingly.

"Pay you for what?" she angrily asked.

"For protecting you," Yohannes replied.

"Protecting me from what? I should call the police for stalking me. It's a crime, you know," she added.

"Maybe you call it a crime here, but from where I am, we call it caring," Yohannes replied, smiling.

"And which planet are you from?" She smiled.

"Africa." Yohannes smiled too, and he extended his hand. "I'm Yohannes. You can call me Johnny."

"Isabella." She shook his hand.

"Arrivederci." Yohannes left her to enjoy her favorite ice cream in The Gelatist.

Yohannes was a likable young man. Isabella wasn't bothered about him following her. On the next weekend, he eagerly waited for her under the Dogali Obelisk. At the usual time, Yohannes saw Isabella coming from a distance. He stepped to the sidewalk and waited for her, wearing his irresistible smile. She smiled back. They walked to The Gelatist together. Ice cream with a gorgeous girl who spoke Italian, Yohannes felt like he was in a utopia.

Fast forward, Isabella and Yohannes hit it off. From the archeological point of view, Yohannes guided Isabella to rediscover her birth city, Rome. Then she introduced him to her family. And on his break from the university, he took her to Paris. As lovers who traveled to Paris do, Yohannes and Isabella placed a padlock on the famous Pont des Arts bridge and threw the key into the Seine river, a symbol of undying commitment to each other.

On Valentine's Day evening, after a romantic dinner, Yohannes took Isabella to Ponte Sant'Angelo, also known as the Bridge of Angels, for a walk. The bridge was known for its romantic stories of marriage proposals. Lovers also affectionately call it the Kissing Destination. Isabella thought the date, the twilight hour, and the location were perfect for Yohannes to propose to her.

"Wow! Love is really in the air tonight," Yohannes said after observing many happy couples enjoying the romantic atmosphere on the bridge.

"Corretto. It's a perfect date and time," Isabella said, holding him tight.

But the golden hour on the bridge was gone before Isabella got what she expected. When they started leaving the bridge, Isabella broke into tears all of a sudden. Yohannes was startled by her sudden emotional meltdown, and he did everything he could to soothe her. Finally,

Isabella confessed that she wanted to get married while her grandma was still alive.

"After our trip to Paris, I was expecting you to propose, and I convinced myself that tonight was the night." Isabella started sobbing again.

Everyone on the bridge was happy, smiling, and laughing. Only his valentine was unhappy and crying. Yohannes felt terrible about it, and he knelt on his knee and took her hand involuntarily. Isabella's mood incredibly changed from blue to happy.

"Isabella, il Mio Amore, will you marry me?" Yohannes asked.

"Si, si!" Isabella jumped with joy.

Yohannes kissed her ring finger and said, "This kiss is a place holder for the ring." She pulled him up and kissed him passionately.

A few weeks later, Isabella and her family began preparing for a small, Italian traditional wedding. Yohannes got out of the pool of love when Isabella took him to visit the church where they were going to get married.

After many sleepless nights, Yohannes decided to run away to Milan on the eve of their wedding. Isabella received a bouquet of yellow flowers and an apology letter on her wedding day from her runaway groom. The incident shocked Isabella and her family.

As part of his charm, Yohannes liked to ask interesting questions and listen more than talking about himself. He didn't want to focus on his own story. He tried to get to know Yared and Ezana on the road, but Tsehay pressed him hard to tell his story of romance in Rome instead.

And both Yared and Ezana loved the story.

They arrived at Lake Hashenge, which was 101 miles away from Mekelle.

"Continua," Yohannes said, pulling his car off the road.

Yared and Ezana were hooked and didn't like that he paused the story on the climax.

"Oh, my God!" Tsehay exclaimed when Lake Hashenge unveiled wide open in front of her. "What a pleasant surprise, Uncle John."

Ezana was expecting a sushi restaurant, so he was confused about what was happening. But he liked the fresh breath around the beautiful lake. Yohannes led them to walk on the green field to the shore of the lake. To the Denver family's surprise, freshly fished fishes were waiting for them. Yohannes greeted his guy who took care of the fishing and introduced him to his guests.

After taking a moment to appreciate the beauty of the lake and its dramatic surrounding landscapes, Yohannes got down to business.

"King Ezana, you requested sushi, and we serve you with something even better: sashimi," Yohannes said, pulling his sleeves up to wash his hands.

"Thank you, Uncle John," Ezana said.

"Uncle John? I'm the only one who calls him that. That's mine." Tsehay giggled.

"Oh, by the way, I'm also named after a great king, Emperor Yohannes IV. You can give me any name around that," Yohannes said.

"Emperor Yohannes?" Ezana asked.

"Why not? Let me be an emperor for today." Yohannes agreed.

After he washed his hands, Yohannes peeled the skins from each fish. He squeezed lemon all over them and sliced them into sashimi. Then he put a local sauce on the side.

"Ecco qui. Mangiarie," Yohannes said, inviting them to eat.

"This is delicious!" Yared said.

"I told you Uncle John is amazing," Tsehay said proudly.

"Tea is good after sashimi. And my mother is an expert in making tea. We're only 18 miles away from Alamata," Yohannes said, beaming.

"I want to see my auntie," Tsehay said.

They walked back to the car and continued their road trip in the same direction to the city of Alamata. Yohannes tried to keep himself away from being the center point of the conversation by asking Yared and Tsehay many questions. But he couldn't avoid it. All they wanted to find out how his relationship with Isabella ended.

"Isabella was so kind. She forgave me after six months. Not only that, but she also surprised me with flowers on my graduation."

"Wow! What a heart of gold," Tsehay said.

"Absolutely! After that, we became like family and kept in touch. When she got married, I offered her and her husband a full package trip to Tigray as a wedding gift. And guess what, their first son was conceived during their ten-day visit here. When their son was born, they asked me to be his godfather. I accepted, and Leonardo is my godson." Yohannes stopped talking and focused on driving when they started descending Grat Kahisu mountain.

"It feels like a great fiction story," Yared said.

"It does," Tsehay agreed.

All digested the story while Yohannes drove down the terrifyingly beautiful hill carefully.

"How about you, Emperor Yohannes? Are you married?" Ezana asked.

"Yes. I have two boys named after our great generals, Alula and Hayelom. And another boy is on the way. His name will be Sihul, after another hero. I'm sure you already know about the names," Yohannes said passionately. "I have a great interest in names."

"So do I," Yared said.

All congratulated Yohannes. Tsehay patted him on the back. Yared and Tsehay were not comfortable enough to push the conversation beyond that. They didn't want Yohannes to ask them about why they didn't have more children.

8

WITH A GREAT NAME COMES
GREAT INSPIRATION

When they arrived in Alamata, the center of Raya's beautiful culture, Yohannes showed them around before he took them to his mother's house. Tsehay was so thrilled to see her auntie after such a long time. Yohannes's mom, an excellent storyteller herself, treated them in a way they would never forget. Everybody liked her special tea and the funny stories she told about the upbringing of her son, Yohannes.

On the way out to the car, Yared and Ezana walked ahead, and Tsehay and Yohannes followed behind. Yohannes got the chance to ask Tsehay if they had a plan for another child or not. She broke down into tears in the middle of trying to explain. He hugged her.

"I'm sorry. I shouldn't have asked you," Yohannes whispered.

"Our son wants a sister or brother. We tried a lot before my dad passed, but I wasn't a good wife in the last two years. It's all my fault." She kept sobbing.

"It's not your fault. It's not anybody's fault." Yohannes gave her a napkin.

To divert Tsehay from the sad topic, Yohannes updated her on his book project titled *Underappreciated Tigrayans* based on the extraordinary lives of ten prominent Tigrayan rebels, leaders, intellectuals, and artists. He told her some of the significant figures

23

included in the book, such as Ra'esi Wolde Selassie, Gebrehiwet Baykedagn, Blata Hailemariam Reda, Gebretsadik WeldeYohannes, and Kiros Alemayehu and kept the rest secret.

"Fun fact, Ra'esi Wolde Selassie wasn't only a brilliant and brave leader, but he was also an avid chess player of the 19th century," Yohannes said, smiling.

"Wow! That's amazing. I can't wait to read this book," Tsehay said.

***

They enjoyed the views of beautiful landscapes and towns on their way back to Mekelle. Ezana asked a million questions about everything he saw, and all the grown-ups in the car were happy to answer.

They made a quick stop in Maychew town to visit Tilahun Gizaw high school, which was named after the revolutionary Tilahun Gizaw.

When his parents talked in the local languages, Ezana always picked up the topics or names and searched them on Google to stay in the know, and he asked questions if he found something interesting.

After he Googled Tilahun Gizaw and found it interesting, Ezana asked Yohannes to tell him more. Yohannes, who went to the school named after Tilahun Gizaw, explained to Ezana how brave Tilahun was, how his significant role in the student movement led to the Ethiopian revolution, and how he got killed by government soldiers while he was accompanying his girlfriend.

They got back to Mekelle late in the evening. Yohannes parked his car in the Aksum Hotel compound and got off to say, *"Ciao,"* to them. Ezana walked toward him for a hug, but Yohannes stopped him.

"I save the best for last, my king," Yohannes said, grinning. Then he hugged Yared and kissed Tsehay goodbye.

"I have no words to thank you enough, Uncle John," Tsehay said.

"I'm speechless too," Yared added.

"I enjoyed you the most. I love you guys," Yohannes said. "Now, please allow me to speak to the king."

Tsehay blew a kiss to him and left with Yared.

"Thank you for waiting, King Ezana," Yohannes said.

"My pleasure, Emperor Yohannes."

"You know, there is a saying that goes like this: 'With great power comes great responsibility.' And with great names like yours and mine come great inspirations. Our parents named us after the great king and emperor to inspire us for similar greatness. Am I making a sense?" Yohannes asked.

"A lot of sense," Ezana said.

"Eccellente! I know your parents are patriots. They know lots of history. Your mom told me that you are going to Aksum soon. Use that opportunity to explore about your namesake, the legendary King Ezana. Enjoy Tigray, the open-air museum."

"Thank you. You're super awesome," Ezana said.

"Welcome to the motherland. I love you." The kings hugged it out.

9

THE SEVEN-YEARS YOUNGER EFFECT

E zana and his parents stayed in Mekelle for a few days. They visited all of their family and friends and all of the landmarks in the city. They saw Emperor Yohannes IV Palace, the Martyr's Memorial Monument, and churches. There wasn't a new site for Tsehay and Yared, but they had to show Ezana all the attractions he knew in his bedtime stories.

During their stay in Mekelle, Rahel Art Gallery became the ideal place for dinner. "Food for the body and the soul," Tsehay liked to call it.

While Yared ordered food and drinks, Tsehay and Ezana look around at the various artworks painted by talented young artists from the city.

After visiting all the major attractions in Mekelle, Ezana preferred staying behind in the hotel room when his parents went out to meet people. Every time Tsehay and Yared came back, Ezana greeted them with complaints about Internet connection and room service.

One evening when his parents came back to the hotel room, Tsehay asked, "How was your day, baby?"

"Boring! Why is everything super slow, the WiFi and the room service?" Ezana said.

"Baby, it's still 2009 here, not 2016. Seven years ago, there was no 4G Internet service, even in the United States," Tsehay said.

"Not only that. According to the Ge'ez calendar, you are seven years younger here, and that makes you five years old. And as a five year old, you are not allowed to use the Internet," Yared said, laughing.

"That's a good point, hun," Tsehay said, giving Ezana a look as if to say, "You better not complain."

Ezana didn't reply to his parents. Instead, he typed "when was 4G service started in the US?" in the Google search bar, and he waited for the slow connection to give him the answer. He was hoping his parents would be wrong so that he could win the argument, but it turned out they were accurate. The service had started in 2009/2010.

As Ezana always did to learn about new subjects, he Googled the Ge'ez Calendar. Then that led him to the Ge'ez Alphabet.

10

LUWAM, THE CHARMING LITTLE GIRL

One day, Tsehay brought her niece to the hotel room to hang out with Ezana. Luwam, the same age as Ezana, was cheerful and fun to be around. Tsehay made a brief intro to each other. Ezana paused the movie he was watching and unplugged his earphones while his mom was doing the introduction. Luwam radiated to hear her auntie complimenting her during the intro.

"Thanks for saying good stuff about me, auntie," Luwam said shyly.

"My pleasure, sweetie. If you get bored here, you can go down for swimming or ice cream or both." She dashed some cash on the coffee table and left the cousins alone.

When Tsehay slammed the door, Luwam turned her face to Ezana to start a conversation, but he was already back on his earphones watching a movie. She didn't give up because Tsehay tipped her off earlier how unhappy about the trip he was. She knew her mission was to make him happy.

First, she tried talking to him, which didn't work. Then she did her trick of acting funny, dancing like crazy, and making impressions of famous characters.

Ezana unplugged his earphones.

Luwam screamed, "Yes! Finally!" and jumped around the room.

Ezana waited until she ended her celebrating.

"Look, you are fantastic, but I'm not in the mood right now. Sorry." Ezana plugged the earphones back in and continued watching.

Luwam's face turned from radiance to darkness in light speed. Her charm usually worked with anyone but failed her with Ezana. She walked to the corner of the room, picked up a landline phone, and dialed zero. When the operator responded, she gave her a phone number and waited on hold until the operator connected her.

Ezana paused the movie and spied her actions. The operator put Luwam's mom on the phone, which made Luwam sparkle again. Since their conversation was in Tigrigna, Ezana couldn't understand much of it, but he knew she was reporting about him. In the middle of the phone conversation, Luwam turned around to Ezana and said one word in particular. Ezana immediately opened Google translate and typed the Tigrigna word. The English translation of the word shocked him.

Luwam finished talking with her mom, banged the phone when she hung up, and slammed the door behind her. Ezana shrugged his shoulder to ignore what she said about him and continued watching the movie. But a blank dialogue box popped in his imaginary head and "jerk," the word that Luwam used to describe him, appeared in it.

11

HARRY POTTER, KERRY WASHINGTON, AND EDDIE MURPHY

Most of the time, Ezana retreated into his comic books, movies, and imaginary dialogues with his superhero friends. One afternoon, Tsehay was going to her parents' elementary school in Mekelle to give books she collected over the years, and she invited Ezana to join her and Yared for the book donation event. He refused and stayed behind in the hotel room to watch movies on *Netflix*. But the WiFi was weak, and he gave up *Netflix* and picked up one of his comic books.

When he started to read, something popped up in his mind. *Hmm, what kind of birthday gift would they give me this time?* he thought. "A few days away to become Harry Potter," he muttered to himself and went back to reading.

His friend, Grace, called him Harry Potter on his birthdays after she found out Ezana shared a birthday with the star of the Harry Potter movies, Daniel Radcliff. They both were born on July 23rd. Grace, a die-hard fan of the British actor, coined the name first, and all of Ezana's family and friends followed. But he wasn't the only one with a star's name in the family.

On a beautiful afternoon of the previous summer in Denver, Ezana, and Yared waited outside for Tsehay to come out from the bathroom.

There was a family concert at the famous Red Rocks Amphitheatre, and Ezana didn't want to miss any of the performances. Tsehay was busy working that entire week, didn't get the chance to go to a beauty salon, and had to do her hair herself.

Yared noticed Ezana's frustration, went into the house, and came back with a Rubik's Cube, a trick he sometimes used to calm Ezana. He challenged him to solve the puzzle in under three minutes for twenty dollars. Ezana accepted the challenge. Yared hoped to see his wife walk out before Ezana won, but Ezana did it before she came out.

He solved the Rubik's Cube in two minutes and forty-two seconds, his second-best time.

Rubbing his thumb against his index and middle fingers to ask for his twenty, Ezana roared in sudden happiness with a wide smirk on his face, "Give me my Harriet Tubman."

Yared slammed the twenty-dollar bill on Ezana's hand. Tsehay came out and got confused when she saw their faces. She expected Ezana would be angry, but she observed the opposite. She found out about the twenty dollars later on the road on their way to the Red Rocks.

"How do I look?" Tsehay asked, borrowing Audrey Hepburn's line from the classic movie Breakfast at Tiffany's.

"Gorgeous!" Yared exclaimed, opening the car's front passenger door for her.

"Just gorgeous? I was expecting like, 'You look as gorgeous as Halle Berry,' or something," Tsehay said, pretending to be a spoiled teenage girl.

Ezana laughed, mocking his mom from the back seat.

"What?" Tsehay questioned Ezana.

"Halle Berry? Give me a break, Mom. Maybe Kerry Washington."

Yared knew Halle Berry but not Kerry Washington. Ezana and Tsehay went through her many movies until he remembered her.

"She is flawless too," Yared said, rechecking his wife.

"She is knockout," Ezana exclaimed and explained Kerry Washington was one of the top ten most beautiful black actresses in Hollywood. Tsehay asked what her exact rank was in the top ten. Ezana Googled and replied that she was at number seven.

"Seventh, not bad, honey," Yared said, laughing.

"And what rank does that put you in, hun? Did you realize that if I'm not Halle Berry, that you can't be Denzel Washington?" Tsehay asked Yared humorously.

"Denzel Washington!" Ezana exploded into a peal of nonstop laughter. Tsehay begged Ezana to match his dad with a Hollywood star.

"Dad looks like Eddie Murphy," Ezana said.

Yared beamed, and a wave of happiness flooded in his body. Tsehay gazed at Ezana, her jaw dropped. The look of disbelief couldn't fade from her face until Ezana spoke again.

"I mean unfunny, Eddie Murphy," Ezana said and closed his eyes with both hands.

Instead of arguing with them, Yared laughed out loud to make his point.

"And where does that put you, baby?" Tsehay asked Ezana. "You know what goes around comes around."

Ezana shrugged. "I favor being smart over being handsome."

Both proud parents nodded at the same time. Ezana enjoyed watching them doing it from behind.

"You are both, baby," Tsehay said.

"That's true. Smart and handsome," Yared agreed.

Yared made right off the main road to ascend toward the Red Rocks Amphitheatre. They could see many cars parked, and the stage light was all over the rocks. While looking for parking, Yared asked Ezana if Eddie and Kerry made a movie together.

"You are getting obsessed about this thing, Dad," Ezana said, googling his dad's question.

Yared got lucky finding parking, and Ezana came up with a movie Eddie Murphy and Kerry Washington acted in together: *A Thousand Words.*

"Great! We'll watch it on Netflix tomorrow," Tsehay said, getting out of the car.

Since then, Ezana would sometimes use the stars' names to call his parents. He would call his dad "Eddie Murphy" when he needed something from him by making him happy.

"Mom, guess who just walked in?" Ezana would say on days when he was not happy with his dad.

When Tsehay shouts back, "Who?"

"Unfunny Murphy," Ezana would say, exploding in laughter.

12

LAND OF THE LEGENDS

Tsehay and Yared rented a four-wheel-drive vehicle in Mekelle and set off for a road trip the next day. The couple agreed to drive in turns. Tsehay had the mornings shift, and Yared had the afternoons. Yared sat comfortably on the front seat and Ezana sat in the back. Tsehay ignited the engine of the car and reminded both to buckle up their seat belts before she rolled out of Aksum Hotel.

"See you soon for Ashenda, Mekellewani," Tsehay said. "I can't wait to transform myself into fully Ashenda girl costume and dance my heart out." Tsehay danced in her car seat.

"You are fired up, Mom."

"I know. Wait until you see it, baby, and you will wish you were a girl. I believe Ashenda is the most beautiful female festival on the planet!"

"I agree," Yared nodded.

"Maybe I should invite Grace sometime in the future. Can foreigners join?" Ezana asked.

"Absolutely! Ashenda is a religious and cultural festival that embraces and promotes freedom and equality for the entire female population," Tsehay said excitedly.

"You are right, hun. We should promote and make this beautiful culture an international festival for all women around the globe," Yared said, mimicking Tsehay's energy.

***

Tsehay took Eyasu Berhe Street, named after the legendary artist, and signaled to the left when she approached near the Mesobo hill.

"Baby, embrace yourself to hear true stories more amazing than your comic superheroes," Tsehay said to Ezana, beaming in excitement as she drove on the road to Tembien Abiy Addi.

"That's true. Get ready to enjoy extraordinary stories narrated by the gorgeous Mama Tsehay," Yared said proudly.

"Featuring the former tour guide, Daddy Yared," Tsehay said, smiling.

They're in an excellent mood, Ezana thought and grinned.

On their first day of the road trip, they cruised to Tembien Abiy Addi, the birthplace of Emperor Yohannes IV and Africa's first general, Alula Aba Nega. It was also rich in history, culture, and nature. Tsehay alerted Ezana to listen to her carefully and described the remarkable history of Emperor Yohannes IV, king of kings of Ethiopia, who defended and ruled Ethiopia for seventeen years.

"Due to his martyrdom in battle defending his country from invaders, Emperor Yohannes IV became The Last King of the World who died on a battlefield," Tsehay said.

"Narrated beautifully," Yared nodded.

"Hun, now it's your turn. Tell Ezana about General Alula before we arrive at Abiy Addi."

Yared asked Ezana if he needed a break before he started a new chapter of history. Ezana was hooked and gave Yared the green light to tell the story.

"Wonderful. It's an honor and pleasure," Yared said. He sat comfortably and cleared his throat. "Young Alula was an ordinary soldier until the day he captured a king in a battle," he began his narration.

"Powerful opening line, Dad," Ezana complimented.

"I know," Tsehay agreed.

Yared, encouraged by their compliments, continued describing the great African general of the 19th century.

"Right after King Tewodros died, King Tekle Giorgis of Wag claimed himself as emperor of Ethiopia. But Dejazmach Kahsay, the future Emperor Yohannes IV, refused to acknowledge him. Then self claimed Emperor Tekle Giorgis marched with thousands of his army to destroy the rebellious Dejazmach. The small but disciplined soldiers of Dejazmach Kahsay confronted the massive army of Emperor Tekle Giorgis at Adwa. After a one day-long battle, the self-claimed emperor was captured by a soldier named Alula. After that victory in Adwa, the victorious soldiers marched to Aksum and witnessed their leader, Dejazmach Kahsay, crowned as Yohannes IV, emperor of Ethiopia.

For Alula, that victory paved the path to greatness. Both the emperor and Alula achieved many victories over foreign invaders and colonizers. Alula's extraordinary bravery and skills rocketed him to become 'The Garibaldi of Abyssinia' and the first army general of Africa," Yared said. And he explained further the general's adventures, including the battle of Dogali, where Alula defeated the Italians, known as the first defeat of the European army by Africans.

Ezana listened curiously and asked many questions in between.

"Wow! But how come Hollywood didn't make movies about them?" Ezana asked at the end.

"That is a great question, son," Yared said. "Maybe one day you will make movies about them."

To show her approval, Tsehay exaggerated her head nod, and she almost hit the steering wheel.

"That means I have to go to film school. Cool."

"Why not? You love movies, anyway, don't you?" Tsehay asked.

"Of course. I love superheroes movies, and these are superhero stories." Ezana's face glowed.

"True stories of real superheroes!" Yared said.

13

I'LL HAVE WHAT WILL SMITH
HAD FOR BREAKFAST

The family checked in at the Mai Lemin Botanical Garden Lodge. Stunned by the beauty of the lodge, Tsehay halted the car in the middle of the opened gate. For a plantswoman like Tsehay, the place appeared to be paradise. She had a small garden at their Denver house but abandoned it after the accidental passing of her father. Yared purposely booked their stay at the Botanical Garden Lodge to please his wife, and it worked excellently.

She froze in awe, appreciating the grace of the place. The garden, made up of several indigenous trees, plants, and colorful flowers, could overwhelm anyone, let alone a plantswoman.

Tsehay's sudden halt and shock confused the guard who stood by the gate, welcoming them in. Yared understood what the guard was thinking. He lowered the car window and informed him of what was happening.

"Ah, I thought she was a lunatic," the guard blundered and smiled sheepishly.

Ezana exploded in laughter. Yared tried not to laugh but couldn't stop himself from chuckling. Their laugh woke Tsehay from her dumbstruck stare.

"Are you laughing at me?" she asked.

The innocent guard flinched and apologized for his indelicate words. "Don't worry, sir," Yared said and tipped him some cash.

Tsehay entered thoroughly into the compound and pulled over in the empty parking lot.

"Thank you, hun," Tsehay said gratefully and pressed a kiss on his cheek.

The family freshened up and visited the historic town of Abiy Addi, and they went to the famous Mai Lemin park for quality time and fresh air. The next day, they enjoyed a beautiful breakfast outside in the garden. Rooms built in traditional cottage style amid captivating fauna and flora with the birds' musical sounds made the lodge seem like a meditation center in a utopia.

Tsehay did a walking meditation in the botanical garden before they headed to Hawzen. Yared and Ezana shared another laugh when they caught the paranoid guard secretly spying on Tsehay.

According to the agreement and the itinerary of the trip, Tsehay took charge of driving and followed the direction to Hawzen. Neither of Ezana's parents knew the newly constructed road from Abiy Addi to Hawzen, but the lodge manager gave them adequate information.

Half an hour into the trip, nobody had talked. They admired the scenic mountains and landscapes. To their right, fascinating chains of mountains ran as far as Gherealta, and to their left, the gorgeous mountains of Nebelet and Adwa were visible.

"Do these mountains have some similarities to the Grand Canyon?" Ezana asked, staring at the Gherealta mountains.

"Breathtaking like the Grand Canyon with spiritual blessings," Yared replied.

"What do you mean?" Ezana asked.

"The highest churches in the world are right on top of these mountains," Yared explained.

"Also known as churches in the sky," Tsehay added.

Ezana started showing interest in stories and sightseeing after his parents planted the filmmaking idea in him. His history enthusiast parents glowed when they sensed his craving and loaded him with exciting stories and explanations to his questions from the previous day's stories of Emperor Yohannes IV and General Alula Aba Nega.

Thousands of stories and millions of photos later, they checked into Gherealta Lodge, Hawzen, for a night. The lodge left its visitors speechless with its superbly built traditional Hidmo rooms with a majestic view of the Gherealta mountains. The family stood at the vast opened compound to feast their eyes on the landscape.

After moments of appreciation, they walked into the lobby. Ezana became intrigued when he saw pictures of Hollywood celebrities like Will Smith and his wife Jada Pinket Smith who visited the area. He never expected Will and Jada, Hollywood's royalty couple, would visit such a place. His mind ran back to his Denver school and imagined how awesome it would be to talk about his exciting connection with the celebrities. But that spark of an idea faded when he remembered what his classmate Liam did last summer.

Ezana was not only attracted by the photos of the Hollywood heavyweights displayed around the lobby but also lost in his imagination and contemplation. The manager of the lodge, who noticed Ezana's particular interest in the images, volunteered himself for any questions.

"I'm a manager here. If you have any questions, feel free to ask me."

Ezana smiled broadly and jumped on the offer without hesitation.

"When did Will Smith and Jada Pinket Smith come here?" Ezana started, and he bombarded the manager with many more questions.

The middle-aged man answered all of his questions the best he could. Tsehay and Yared put their luggage in their room and came back for Ezana. They waited by the corner until Ezana finished, and his parents apologized to the manager for all of Ezana's questions.

"I like his inquisitiveness," the manager said. "And I want to make him happy. Please follow me."

He led and showed them the room where the Smith family stayed, and Ezana's entire body radiated. They took some pictures of Ezana in the room. Then, to Ezana's amazement, the manager told them they were upgraded into the Smiths' suite without any extra charge.

Will Smith's quote, *"It feels like God visits everywhere else but lives in Africa,"* was engraved on wood and hung on the wall of the room. Ezana became ecstatic. Tsehay and Yared thanked the manager.

When the manager left, Yared closed the door and turned to Ezana, electrified.

"Congratulations, son! You've got a big story to tell when you get back in school!" he yelled.

"Yes, a huge story," Tsehay shouted from the bathroom.

Ezana shrugged and sunk into one of the traditional chairs in the room.

"What?" Yared asked, losing some flames of his excitement.

Tsehay rested her ear on the door to listen from the bathroom.

"You know Liam, right?" Ezana asked his dad.

"Liam, the cool white kid...what about him?"

"Yeah, you know his dad is kind of a movie guy, and he took him to Hollywood during the premiere of the movie *Once Upon a Time in Hollywood*. Liam met all the stars and the director of the film. And do you know who the stars and the director were?"

"Who?" Yared asked.

"Leonardo DiCaprio, Brad Pitt, Margot Robbie, Al Pacino... Quentin Tarantino," Tsehay whispered to herself in the bathroom.

"You have no idea how huge celebrities those people are. Mom knows them. Right, Mom?"

"They are huge!" she yelled.

"Will Smith is one of the greatest and the coolest Hollywood stars for sure, but when you compare this with Liam's story, this is just interesting trivia," Ezana said.

Yared shrugged and told Ezana it was only a few days into their long vacation, and he would have a story worth presenting by the end of their trip.

They woke up early the next morning to enjoy the view of the sunrise over the majestic mountains of Gherealta. They were lucky to go out for the panorama before breakfast. It was about to rain. The beauty of the mountains was replaced by the grace of slow-moving clouds.

"A good day starts with a coffee" was Yared's favorite motto. He said it almost every day. Ezana liked to mimic his dad with the slogan he invented: *"An awesome day starts with a bowl of cereal."* And Tsehay preferred, *"A great day starts with a smile,"* and she said it with a sparkling smile.

Tsehay smiled, Yared yawned for coffee, and Ezana was craving cereal. The smells of freshly baked bread and coffee were coming out from the breakfast room, and it was easy to locate it. The manager welcomed them in his uniformed smile. Once again, he pleased Ezana by providing him choices of breakfasts, including Will Smith's favorite.

"I like to have what Will Smith had for breakfast," Ezana announced.

Will Smith's preference was assembled by himself from both local and continental breakfasts: cheese omelet with local honey, toasted himbasha, and freshly squeezed juice. Ezana enjoyed it and made a mental note about it.

14

THE FIRST HIJRA OF ISLAM

The family drove beneath the majestic mountains of Gherealta toward the town of Wukro. They made quick stops at the churches of Abraha we Atsbeha and Wukro Cherkos, among the oldest and the best rock-hewn churches of Tigray. Then they headed in the direction of Adigrat and stopped to visit one of the landmarks under the sky of the open-air museum.

The historical Mosque of Al Nejashi, believed to be one of the first mosques in Africa built by the companions of Prophet Muhammad, was conveniently located on the route. After the visit of the ancient and historical mosque, Yared and Tsehay described the story of how Prophet Muhammad's first followers, the Sahabah, fled from the persecution of the ruling Quraysh tribe of Mecca and sought refuge in the Christian Kingdom of Aksum. Ezana was intrigued by the story, and his parents went deeper into the beautiful part of the story.

In the migration to Abyssinia, also known as the first hijra, were a group of fifteen men and women, including Ruqayyah bint Muhammad, the daughter of Prophet Muhammad. The prophet told his followers that the just king of Aksum would take good care of them in his friendly country, and that's what exactly King Armah of Aksum did. He welcomed them warmly, provided them shelter and food, and let them stay as long as they wanted.

But when the Quraysh learned the followers of Prophet Muhammad could harmlessly practice their faith in the Christian Kingdom, they sent a delegation to the king to demand the return of the fugitives. Members of the delegation gave gifts to generals of the kingdom to get access to the king. They presented expensive gifts to the king and begged him to hand over the exiles who invented a foolish religion they had never heard of before. King Armah listened to the appeal of the Meccans but refused to grant them what they demanded before he listened to the side story of the people who sought his protection.

King Armah called the refugees to his chamber and let them describe their new religion called Islam. The king listened from his heart to the point that he cried. Then King Armah returned the gifts to the Quraysh Meccans and let the followers of Prophet Muhammad practice their religion freely in his kingdom. Since then, the companions of the prophet have lived and practiced their faith in the kingdom.

They built a mosque, and some of them remained until their deaths.

"Are you telling me that Islam was welcomed here before, even in Saudi Arabia?" Ezana asked after he listened to the history in awe.

"That's true," Tsehay said.

Yared nodded and grinned happily that his boy listened and grasped the essence of the story.

15

THIS IS HOW WE DISCIPLINE
OUR KIDS IN AFRICA

The family road trip continued to Adigrat. Ezana's parents tried hard to make the road trip as enjoyable as possible by telling Ezana the heroic stories of Dejazmach Sabagadis Woldu, who governed Tigray, measured the depth and the coastline of the red sea, and was one of the prominent governors of 19th-century Ethiopia.

They wrapped up their journey by stopping for Belles—a cactus pear treat on the skirts of Adigrat. It was raining the whole morning, and the Belles were so cold, so fresh. It was perfect timing to enjoy the tasty fruit. Ezana was amazed by how cheap it was compared to the U.S. price.

Yared replaced Tsehay at the steering wheel. Tsehay, before she sat back and relaxed, turned around and checked if Ezana buckled up. He was on point. She smiled at him and stared at the road in front of her.

"Good to go," Tsehay said.

Ezana, still thinking about the low price of the cactus pear, created two dialogue balloons in his head, one for his dad and the other for himself. After he ran the question and answer in his mind, he decided to ask his dad.

"Dad?"

"Yes?"

"Why don't you export cactus pears to the U.S.?" Ezana asked.

"That's a great idea. I'll consider it," Yared said.

Ezana put his hand over his mouth and made a coughing sound to mask his laughter.

"He replied as you expected, didn't he?" Tsehay asked, giggling.

"Precisely," Ezana said and laughed out loud.

"What?" Yared asked.

Tsehay and Ezana laughed together. Yared shrugged and focused on driving carefully on a busy road emerging from Adigrat, the beautiful city of Agame.

Arrived in the city of Adigrat, and Yared stopped to ask for directions. While he was looking for somebody, Tsehay saw traffic police coming toward them.

"Is he coming to us, hun? What did you do?"

"Nothing," Yared said, making sure he didn't do anything wrong.

The police advanced and stopped on the driver's side. Yared lowered his window. Ezana did the same at his back seat window, eager to see what would happen.

"What did I do wrong, officer?" Yared asked.

"How are you?" the police asked, ignoring Yared's question. He gave Tsehay a polite nod with a smile.

"Oh, we are doing well. Thank you," Yared said.

"And we just arrived," Tsehay added, grinning broadly.

"I noticed. May I help you with something?" the police asked.

Knowing nothing exciting would happen, Ezana leaned back in his seat.

"Yes, please," Yared said. He turned to his wife. "What was the name of the hotel? It's in the Bible."

Tsehay pulled her cell phone from her handbag and retrieved the information from her email account.

"It's Canaan," Tsehay said.

The police gave them the directions using his hands, chin, and words.

"And if you want to try Tihlo and Mess, ask anyone for Geza Tegaru. You'll enjoy the best Tihlo and Mess in town," the police said, departing.

"Geza Tegaru. Loved it already. Thank you, sir," Tsehay said, bowing.

"We appreciate that. Thank you!" Yared shouted.

"What a friendly officer!" Tsehay said.

"He was the exact opposite of what I heard about African cops. I'm disappointed," Ezana said, chuckling.

Tsehay asked Ezana what he heard, and Ezana told a story that he heard from a Nigerian boy in school.

"A girl born and raised in America went to Lagos to spend her summer vacation with her grandparents. She met a Nollywood actress on her flight to Nigeria, and because of her eccentric charisma, she became friends with many Nigerian celebrities. Soon, she was on top of all the Nollywood party lists.

"The girl's conservative, protestant grandparents didn't like the party marathons and her wild manners. They warned her to behave, but she didn't listen to them. She kept partying and coming home in the mornings.

"One day, the grandpa couldn't take it anymore, so he pulled out his belt and chased her around the house. She managed to lock herself up in a room and call 911 before he spanked her.

"Three policemen arrived at the house. They put the girl in the living room with her grandparents and asked them what happened. She got the chance to explain first. Emotionally sputtering, she exaggerated her innocence and her grandparents' weirdness. The grandparents, when their turn came, told their version of the story calmly.

"The police officers, furious about the girl's wild manners and lack of respect for the old folks, took a moment alone outside and discussed the matters. They went back into the house, two of them put the girl on a table on her stomach, and the third one spanked her until she cried out loud.

"'This is Africa, and this is how we discipline our kids,' the police said," Ezana concluded.

Tsehay and Yared exploded in a peal of nonstop laughter.

"That's a great joke, Ezu," Yared said, ending his laughter.

"That's not a joke. That's a true story, Dad."

"True or not, it's funny," Yared said.

"It's here, Canaan International Hotel!" Tsehay shouted, pointing her finger at a billboard.

Yared flashed a signal to the left, and they saw the hotel on a beautiful cobblestone road. The friendly staff, the cleanliness, and hospitality of the hotel left the family in awe.

"Impressive! Now I know why TripAdvisor rated you four-star," Tsehay murmured.

16

LIFE WITHOUT GOOGLE, GOOGLE MAP, AND WIKIPEDIA

In the first week of the vacation, Tsehay and Yared discovered their son's Internet addiction. Ezana whined and moaned severely whenever the quality of the Internet connection didn't serve him well. His parents kept reminding him to unplug from the Internet so that he could connect with the real world around him.

"It's my birthday week, and it's supposed to be fun. I didn't sign up for this *discovery channel* road trip," he said once, frustrated.

When they entered their family suite at the hotel, Ezana switched on and connected his tablet to the hotel WiFi. Suddenly, he beamed.

Tsehay unpacked their luggage, put out casual clothes for everyone, and reminded Ezana to freshen up and get ready to go.

"Please, Mom!" Ezana said. "I like to stay here. Order something for me to eat on your way out."

Tsehay gave him a look and vanished into the restroom. Ezana knew what that look meant. She gave him that look when she wanted to tell him, "Don't even think about it!" without letting her husband hear what was going on because it also meant "Your father won't like this." That was the redline Ezana couldn't cross.

Against his will, he plugged his tablet in to charging and left for dinner with his parents.

Yared left his car key with a young man who waited outside to wash his car and asked one of the hotel guards for directions. They walked the cobblestoned block from the hotel and merged onto the main asphalt road. They turned left and continued walking down to the heart of the city. As the guard said, they crossed the asphalt when they reached Agazi High School. They marched on attractive cobblestoned alleys and asked for directions a couple of times.

"You can't ignore a restaurant recommendation from a police officer," Yared said to break the silence.

"An extra nice police officer," Tsehay said and looked at Ezana, expecting him to say something. Ezana was busy creating dialogue balloons inside his head, talking with his imaginary friends in his world.

One of Abrehet Abdu's great songs was playing inside a small music shop, and two speakers stationed on both sides of the door made the music reach farther. Yared liked Abreht's music, and he walked into the music shop involuntarily. A young girl inside the shop turned the music down to hear what he was asking. Then she walked outside to give him directions. When Yared started pacing, the music volume went up, and he used it as a soundtrack for his brisk walking.

"Dad, we have Google maps for directions and Google, Wikipedia, and YouTube for any questions, you know. When you were young and curious, what did you have? Whom did you ask?" Ezana asked.

Both Tsehay and Yared nodded, appreciating the question.

"That's a fascinating and interesting question," Yared said, buying time to compose his answer.

Knowing what his dad was trying to do, Ezana nodded, smiled, and gave him time.

"We had teachers, wise men and women, and elders," Yared said. "We used to go to one of them every time a question popped up in our heads."

Ezana nodded. After a few steps, he looked up at his dad and asked if the teachers, the wise men and women, and elders could answer all of their questions.

"Yes," Yared said. "We didn't have that many complex questions, anyway."

17

GEZA TEGARU

Yared asked one more time for directions before they located the famous Geza Tegaru restaurant. Paintings by amateur artists and people dining and drinking made the restaurant attractive, warm, and cozy.

Unlike Yared, Tsehay liked the smell of coffee more than the drink. As soon as they entered the restaurant, she smelled the distinctive aroma of fresh coffee. Tsehay spotted the woman responsible for the fresh smell of coffee. Dressed in white and glowing, the woman roasting on a traditional coffee set in the corner of the restaurant wasn't difficult to locate.

"I already love it," she said, elated.

A friendly waiter welcomed them, shaking their hands, and led them to an empty table for four. The waiter left them with a menu and went to get their drink orders. They saw the waiters serving mouthwatering dishes and wanted to order a couple more foods on top of the main course, Tihlo.

"I'm glad you came, baby," Tsehay whispered to Ezana. "You know, leaving Adigrat without eating Tihlo is like leaving Paris without visiting the Eiffel Tower."

"Hahaha, you're exaggerating, Mom."

While focused on the menu, a familiar voice awoke them.

"Oh! I'm glad to see you again."

Tsehay, Yared, and Ezana looked up in the direction of the voice. Ezana recognized the policeman first. He changed his police uniform and took a moment for Tsehay and Yared to identify him.

"Please join us," Yared said cordially.

"Yes, please have a seat." Tsehay cleared her purse from the fourth chair for him.

Still grinning broadly, the police officer joined them with exciting energy.

Ezana's dead mood came to life again. He liked it when strangers joined them. "New characters," he called them. New conversations with new characters gave him chances to know new stuff about his parents.

"It's a pleasant surprise. We are glad to see you again," Yared said.

"Likewise. My wife owns this restaurant," the policeman announced proudly.

"Oh!" Tsehay and Yared shouted at the same time, beaming even more.

"Congratulations!" Tsehay said.

"It's a wonderful restaurant. Great job," Yared added.

The police officer stood and bowed twice to thank them. He stopped one of the waitresses flying by and whispered something in her ear. The waitress disappeared into the kitchen and came back with complimentary appetizers. The officer took a bite and encouraged them to eat using exaggerated body language to portray the deliciousness of the appetizers.

"Excuse me, officer," Ezana said, looking at the officer quizzically.

Everyone turned to him with broad smiles.

"Is it legal to promote your restaurant while you were in uniform?" Ezana asked.

Tsehay froze, and Yared almost spluttered. The officer laughed and wiped his mouth with a napkin.

"Sorry, officer, in America—" Yared tried to explain.

The policeman interrupted him. "No, it's okay. I liked the question. My name is Fitsum, by the way. What's your name, kid?"

"Ezana."

"Ezana, as a police officer, my job is to serve the public in any way possible. Giving accurate information is one. Are you following me, kid?"

"Yes, sir."

"Good, good kid. When I saw you arrive in our city, I believed you needed to experience Tihlo and Mess, and I suggested the best restaurant in town for your best experience." He stopped and gazed at all of them.

Tsehay and Yared, both with mouths full, nodded.

"I would still recommend you come here if my wife didn't own this restaurant. So, wait until you dine, and then you'll judge me. Deal?" the policeman asked Ezana.

"Great answer, and we have a deal, Mr. Fitsum," Ezana said, giving two thumbs up.

The friendly policeman got up from his seat and kissed Ezana on his forehead. "I'll be back," he said, grinning, and then he vanished into the kitchen and came back with a charming woman.

"My wife, Makda," the policeman introduced her to them proudly.

Tsehay and Yared stood at the same time to shake hands with the policeman's wife. *They did it again*, Ezana thought when his parents stood up together like a choreographed act. And he stood up to shake hands too, but the policeman's wife kissed him on both cheeks instead.

Makda was busy in the kitchen. To save her time, her husband had told her about the guests while coming from the kitchen. She welcomed them cheerfully, took the menu from their table, and told them not to worry about what to order.

Ezana asked Fitsum how his wife got into the restaurant business. Tsehay and Yared turned from Ezana to the policeman, hoping the question wouldn't make him uncomfortable.

To their surprise, they saw Fitsum transform into euphoric. He leaned forward and proudly narrated how Makda began as a shoeshine teen girl and became a successful restauranteur and building owner in Adigrat. The way he told the story was so intriguing that even people sitting next to them were listening.

"I'm sorry. You must be starving. Let me get your orders. It should be ready now." The policeman dashed to the kitchen.

"What a brilliant wife!" Tsehay exclaimed in pride.

"Inspiring success story," Yared added.

Fitsum came back with their food, and Makda followed him with their drinks, the traditional Mess. A combo of Tihlo, Injera, and various kinds of Tsebhi were served on a large tray.

"You see how my love, Makda, is a great chef? She put Tihlo, the main dish in the middle, and other popular dishes around it. Isn't she great?" Fitsum asked them, smiling.

"Stop it," Makda said adorably. "Don't listen to him. He likes to exaggerate."

"He's right. It's so beautiful!" Tsehay said, smiling and nodding.

"I have never seen anything as mouthwatering as this!" Yared said.

"Now, don't listen to my husband. Just eat. I'll send you more Injera." Makda went back, waving hello to some of her customers on her way.

The food looked and tasted great. Ezana ate more Tihlo than he ever did before. Tsehay and Yared washed their delicious food down with their Mess, and Ezana got a Coke.

"My husband liked you a lot, so everything is on the house," Makda said in the end. She refused to accept payment and disappeared into her kitchen without giving them a chance to argue.

"No, don't even think about it!" the policeman insisted when they tried to resist and pay.

18

UNIVERSAL CULTURE

W hat a lovely and amazing couple!" Tsehay said on their way back to the hotel.

"They are! I enjoyed the story, the food, and everything but..." Yared hesitated to finish the sentence.

Ezana already started looking for words to finish Yared's sentence in his head. While he was searching for the right words to make a sound sentence, Tsehay asked Yared to finish it.

"Do you think maybe he paid for our bill because of what Ezana asked?" Yared asked.

"I don't think so. Didn't you see how open, real, and kind the couple were? I think the policeman liked Ezana's honest questions,"Tsehay said.

Yared thought the policeman and his wife were kind and hospitable enough to them and shouldn't have paid their bill. Silence took place, and they all walked, listening to their footsteps and some music in the background.

"I heard some people speaking a different language in the restaurant," Ezana said, breaking the silence.

"You are right, baby. I heard them too. They were members of the Irob people, and they were communicating in their language, Saho. If you are lucky, you might also experience Kunamigna of the Kunama people in west Tigray," Tsehay explained.

"Cool. I'll Google about both the Irob and Kunama people when we get in the room," Ezana said, giving them heads up that he will be online.

Tsehay felt Ezana's enthusiasm reviving and smiled. When they entered the last intersection to the hotel, Ezana broke the silence again.

"Dad, you seemed bothered. What was wrong with the question I asked?"

Tsehay and Yared were lost replaying the scenes from the restaurant in their heads. They both asked him what he said. Ezana took advantage of the moment and rephrased his question.

"What was wrong with the question I asked the policeman? I noticed you both sound uncomfortable every time I ask questions. What's the matter?"

Tsehay wasn't ready to reply, so she turned to Yared.

"That's a great question," Yared said, buying time to formulate his idea.

"Well, you know, in America, it's okay to ask anything. You're appreciated for being inquisitive. But here, our culture is a little different," Yared said, avoiding the specific question about the policeman.

"Is there anything wrong with the questions I ask? For instance, what I asked the policeman was it wrong?"

"No, baby, nothing wrong at all," Tsehay shook her head, even though it was difficult to see the gesture in the dark.

"No. You didn't ask any wrong questions. It was just about the culture," Yared said in a kind of tone that ended the conversation. But Ezana wasn't convinced.

"No matter whether it's right or wrong, the right to ask questions should be a universal culture, Dad," Ezana said casually.

Tsehay and Yared saw each other, and both agreed with what he said.

"Look! Look!" Ezana shouted, pointing his fingers at a monumental cross landmark. The cross was there on the same hill when they walked on the same street earlier to the restaurant, but now, it was lit and glowing gracefully on the mountain. Ezana stopped, facing the cross, and contemplated how it was made. He ran into his mind's storage to compare it to the one he saw in Mekelle. Tsehay and Yared came from behind and hugged him on both sides.

"Awesome. I didn't expect to see another one after the one in Mekelle," Ezana said.

Yared took the opportunity to explain Meskel, a Christian holiday, celebrated colorfully in both cities annually.

It was 10:00 P.M., but the hotel lobby was lively. The coffee machine was on, making that good coffee making sound. When they entered, the pleasant aroma of coffee received them. Yared was tempted to sit for a cup of coffee, but Tsehay reminded him of their early morning schedule.

Climbing the stairs to their second-floor room, Ezana stopped and turned and stared at his parents, who following from behind.

"You all right, baby?" Tsehay asked, concerned.

"I think Fitsum and Makda are the Romeo and Juliet of this city. I hope you guys learned something from them." He turned around and continued climbing faster.

Tsehay and Yared froze for a while and burst into awkward laughter.

"Honey, do you think he noticed our situation?" Tsehay asked.

"No. You know your son. That was nothing but classic Ezana," Yared said to comfort her.

The next morning, they skipped breakfast in the hotel for a chance to explore another place. While Tsehay was warming up the engine, Yared gathered information from the hotel guards on where to go for breakfast, which was not far from the hotel.

Tsehay parked in front of the café, and the family sat outside at the veranda. Ezana preferred scrambled eggs with orange juice. The couple went for Ful, a freshly made spicy breakfast with coffee and tea for drinks.

Before they say goodbye to Adigrat, they stopped for quick cold fresh Belles fruits.

19

WHY ARE WOMEN NOT ALLOWED IN MONASTERIES?

B uckle up, guys. Now I'm ready to face the uphill climb," Tsehay said, excited.

"You are bragging, Mom," Ezana said, laughing.

Yared nodded, agreeing with Ezana while fastening his seat belt. Tsehay ignored their reaction. She crossed herself in prayer as she always did before starting the engine. "In the name of the Father, the Son, and the Holy Spirit. Amen."

She didn't talk for almost half an hour until she finished driving up the strenuous hill. None of them tried to speak to her either.

Yared remembered something and beamed. So excited, he asked Ezana to pass him his laptop bag from the back seat. Yared searched and found the small device he wanted after unzipping and zipping several small pockets in his bag. Then he plugged the flash memory card of Tigrigna music collection, which he bought from a small music store at Kedamay Woyane market in Mekelle.

Timeless ballads started to flow from the front and back speakers of the vehicle. Young and veteran Tigrigna music legends saved them from the uncomfortable silence during the terrifying uphill drive.

Tsehay turned down the volume of the music when she made it safely to the top of the hill. "Thank God," she breathed.

The intense atmosphere cleared for another half an hour. Ezana mocked her on how she looked when ascending the steep hill, and Yared sided with Ezana. When she started driving the downhill at Mount Mugulat, Tsehay became serious and nervous again. Driving downhill appeared to be scarier than uphill.

Tsehay turned herself on mute again and focused on driving safely. The road served all kinds of cars, from small automobiles to big trucks. All drivers were supposed to be slow, alert, and courteous to each other all the time. Big trucks with trailers made the trek safely, applying patience, skill, and caution. Small cars stopped and let the big ones go through first. The downhill slope, an incredible scene with spectacular landscapes, could send chills down to the spines of experienced drivers, let alone for tourists like Tsehay.

To protect Ezana from vertigo, Yared turned the volume of the music up and he distracted Ezana by showing varieties of strangely shaped mountains and impressive views.

After she made it safely to the ground on the other side of the hill, Tsehay pulled over and got out of the car. Yared and Ezana followed her. She put her right hand on her forehead to shield her eyes from the morning sun and looked back at the zigzag road. *It's even more terrifying to look at it than driving down*, she thought.

"It's mind-blowing," Ezana said. "I didn't realize how dangerous that was."

Tsehay nodded. "That's what exactly I felt."

"Great job, honey. Proud of you," Yared said, looking at the hazardous road.

Ezana gave her two thumbs up. She gave him a big hug and didn't let him go until Yared got back in the car and honked the car horn for "Let's go." Tsehay left her anxiety behind. Her great mood came back. She turned the music volume up and sang with every song that came along.

Yared marveled over his wife's sudden change of mood. He turned around to his son and noticed the same feeling on his face. Then Yared winked and smiled at him. Ezana smiled back, but not his innocent smile. Yared knew he did that when he thought something prankish.

"Why did you wink at me, Dad?" Ezana shouted so that his mom could hear him. "Do you have something to tell Mom?"

Yared expected it and laughed out loud. Tsehay turned the volume down to ask them what was going on.

"Dad has something to say, I think."

Tsehay gave Yared a look to spit it out, but he shook his head while laughing.

"I think you were loud, Mom and Dad didn't like your voice," Ezana said mockingly.

Tsehay shrugged and put the volume back to maximum and kept singing until they stopped to donate some cash for the historical monastery church of Debre Damo in a small town called Bizet.

"Honey, who did this small town remind you?" Tsehay asked.

"Berhane Meskel Reda," Yared said without thinking about it. "How about you?"

Tsehay shifted the gear and pressed the brake to slow down the car.

"I was about to say the same. Kahsay Abreha mentioned him and this town in his book many times."

Ezana didn't understand the topic. He waited on the edge of his seat to get out.

"Ezu, you know Kahsay Abreha, the pharmacist from Denver?"

"Yes, Alula's and Kaleb's dad," Ezana replied, and then he realized something. "Now, I know why he named one of his sons Alula."

"And you will soon know why he called his other son Kaleb, after the great king of the Aksumite Kingdom," Tsehay said. She described to Ezana Kahsay Abraha's past revolutionary life and the book he wrote.

Ezana was amazed by the remarkable life behind a pharmacist who lived in Denver. Then Ezana asked about the other guy they mentioned.

"Berhane Meskel Reda was one of the prominent revolutionary leaders of the 1970s in Ethiopia," Tsehay said.

Before they hit the road, Yared pointed out Debre Damo Monastery, also known as Island in Sky and explained to his son about the rich and ancient monastery built atop a mountain table in the 6th century. Yared talked further about the monastery that is accessible only by way of a leather rope up and solely for men.

"Why accessible only for men?" Ezana asked when they got back into the car.

Tsehay nodded in appreciation for Ezana's question.

"This one excludes women, and women's monasteries exclude men," Yared said and tried to skip the topic by showing him at the mountain table, the home of the Abuna Aregawi Damo Monastery from another dimension.

"Dad, what's the reason behind excluding women or men for that matter?"

Yared scratched his hair, contemplating how to explain to him. Tsehay knew when Yared felt uncomfortable by Ezana's questions. She tried to help him by diverting their son's focus to the mountains of Adwa.

"Look how breathtaking that view is," Tsehay said.

"Great view. Let's take some pictures before we miss it," Yared snapped.

They stopped to take pictures of the majestic mountains of Adwa, also known as the Mountains in Conference.

"About the exclusion of men and women in the monastery, Dad," Ezana reminded his dad when they got back in the car.

Tsehay burst into laughter.

Ezana ignored his mom's laugh, kept his cool, and waited for his dad to speak up.

"Oh, boy." Yared sighed. "Monks become monks to dedicate themselves to serve God and pray for world peace. To do so, they stay focused and stay away from distractions. Therefore, monasteries exclude one gender to avoid temptations and distractions." To indicate the conversation was over, Yared turned his face away, opened his bottled water, and took long sips.

"What kinds of temptations and distractions, Dad?" Ezana asked again, carefully presenting it as an innocent question.

Yared halted sipping the water and looked at Tsehay.

"Don't go there, hun. He's playing you. He knows it already." She laughed.

"Mom!" Ezana yelled from the back seat.

Tsehay put the music volume up and continued singing.

20

THE ACCIDENT

A few miles before the town of Enticho, Yared spotted a school sign named after Bashay Awalom. He didn't know that existed and shouted as he discovered it for the first time. Tsehay wrote a paper on the double-agent spy back in college, and Yared knew she would be interested. He was right. She lit up like a candle, which made Yared more excited and distracted him from looking at the road.

"Dad, Dad!" Ezana screamed from the back seat, pointing his fingers at the road through the front glass.

A donkey was crossing the street, but Yared didn't see him in time to slow down or apply the brake to stop. Tsehay screamed when she saw how vulnerable the donkey was. Yared was driving sixty kilometers per hour, and he knew the chance to stop was zero.

A big bang was the next thing they all heard.

The donkey was crossing the road slowly. Yared turned the steering wheel all the way, missed the donkey by inches, but then he couldn't control the car. Three of them looked at the slope in front of them and closed their eyes, screaming.

Amazingly, the car crashed into a big tree off the road at the edge of the slope. They didn't see the tree when the car was speeding up, and none of them expected to make it out alive.

A man holding a stick came running toward the scene of the accident. Yared guessed he was the owner of the donkey.

"Are you guys all right?" the man asked in a trembling voice.

Yared checked Ezana and Tsehay. They seemed okay, except for the shock.

When Yared told him they were well, the man looked up to the sky and said, "This is a miracle. Thank god."

Tsehay, still shocked, just shook her head and reached out to Ezana's hand. Then she praised the Lord for saving them.

Yared got out of the car. He found the bumpers and headlights dropped on the ground. Otherwise, everything looked fine. The man helped Yared lift the dismantled parts of the car, tie them temporarily, and push the Toyota back to the asphalt.

When the car was okay to go, the man apologized for the inconvenience and thanked them for sparing his donkey's life. The man was sympathetic and so humble. They did their best to convince him that it wasn't his or the donkey's fault but an accident.

To make him feel better, they all took a picture together with the donkey and the car. After shaking hands for a goodbye, they got in the car and continued their journey. The man waved to them until the car disappeared from his sight. Ezana did the same to him from the back seat.

"What a super cool man," Ezana said, turning back his face to the front.

Tsehay and Yared shook their heads. Ezana knew both were still in shock, and he wanted to clear the air. He threw a question at them about a specific Tigrigna word the man repeated several times.

"Miracle," Yared answered.

"He meant a miracle saved us," Tsehay explained.

"I couldn't agree more," Ezana said. "And did you guys see his tshirt?"

"No," Yared said.

"What about it?" Tsehay asked.

"His t-shirt has Bill Gates on it. Isn't it funny?" Ezana laughed.

"Bill Gates is not only an ultra-rich man but also the most generous philanthropist. A great friend to Africa," Yared said.

"That's true, but still, it has some humor," Tsehay agreed.

"The man might be materially poor, but he's morally rich," Yared argued.

Ezana planned to cheer his parents up, not drag them into an argument. He withdrew from the topic by asking his mom to pass him a bottle of water from the mini cooler.

At Enticho, Yared asked for a mechanic and parked the car inside a garage for a quick adjustment. The mechanic asked for fifteen minutes to fix the vehicle, but Yared assumed it would take at least half an hour.

They walked out of the garage and sat by the street for a short tea break.

While enjoying their street tea and coffee at the birthplace of Bashay Awalom Haregot, Yared tried to grab Ezana's attention and tell him about the great double-agent spy of the 19th century, but Ezana was indulged in the street activities. He observed tailors sewing outside their shop doors. Mothers were going to market and coming back with something on their hands.

He scanned everything and stared at a foosball game street kids played. He never saw someone playing the game efficiently like them. They were too fast, too furious, and too dramatic. Ezana wondered why they were so fierce like they were in the Olympics.

They went back to the auto mechanic garage in half an hour. The car was fixed and ready.

21

YEHA, LOVE IS IN THE AIR

After they passed the Bon Voyage sign at the exit of Enticho, the breathtaking Adwa mountains unveiled themselves close up. Tsehay and Yared's eyes popped out at the view of the mountains. Tsehay asked Yared to pull over for pictures. He hesitated twice before he finally spotted a perfect place for great pictures.

Ezana questioned why the mountains were called "Mountains in Conference."

Yared pointed out how the giant mountains gracefully sat on a flat landscape. "If you look at the nature of the plateau and the positions of the mountains, they don't seem they belong here but came from other places for a conference."

Tsehay laughed, watching how Yared was describing using his whole body. She took some pictures and selfies until the father-son discussion came to an end. Several photos later, they got back in the car and cruised ahead.

"I feel my whole body laughing," Yared said. "Any idea why, honey?"

"Yeha!" Tsehay exclaimed, giving him a flirtatious glance.

Ezana was scrolling his phone, looking at the pictures they took. He missed noticing the exceptional moment that took place between his parents.

Tsehay kept warning Yared every time she saw animals crossing the road. When she spotted another donkey coming out of a narrow alley to cross the street, she screamed and held his arm at the same time.

"Don't worry, darling. I saw it," Yared said, slowing down to stop the car.

The loaded donkey and his owner, a woman who also carried stuff on her head, crossed from the right side to the left side of the road safely. The woman turned around to face the car and thanked them for their courtesy.

"The donkey passed safely, and the considerate woman is happy," Yared said, moving forward.

Even though Ezana missed the turning point of his parents' sudden change from feeling low to feeling on top of the world, he put his phone away while yielding to the donkey and noticed their over-the-moon mood.

"Speaking of a donkey," Ezana said, laughing and leaning toward his parents, "I think you guys are relaxed enough to hear this out."

"Pretty much relaxed," Tsehay said, grinning broadly.

"We're listening, King Ezana!" Yared shouted.

Ezana hesitated to say what was in his mind, but after Yared addressed him as "King Ezana," he knew it was safe to say anything.

Ezana remembered his dad rarely called him that, like when he won the lottery. He didn't understand where the unusual delight came from, but he liked it. While Ezana was pondering, Tsehay thought he changed his mind and encouraged him to proceed with whatever was on his mind.

"Spit it out, son," Yared said, looking at him through the rearview mirror.

"You almost killed yourself, Dad." Ezana exploded in laughter.

Tsehay and Yared didn't get it. They waited until he finished laughing to hear what cracked him to roar like that. Ezana described how Yared liked the comparison of himself to Eddie Murphy. And Eddie played Donkey in the Shrek movies.

"You are Eddie. Eddie is a donkey in Shrek, and you were about to kill a donkey. So technically, you almost killed yourself." Ezana burst into laughter again.

Tsehay got it and struggled not to laugh.

"Is this supposed to be funny?" Yared asked.

"That's why you are the not funny Eddie Murphy, Dad."

Tsehay couldn't hold it, and she laughed hard with Ezana. Yared had no choice but to join them. Ezana stopped, but they continued chuckling, looking at each other. He watched them from behind, and he didn't remember the last time he saw them genuinely happy like that.

"We're almost there," Yared said, pointing his finger at something to show Tsehay. She clapped passionately.

Ezana leaned forward and tried to see what was ahead. He saw a small sign on the right side of the road but couldn't read it. He asked what that was, and both of his parents shouted, "Yeha!" That didn't make any sense to him. He leaned back and waited for the mystery to unfold.

Yared signaled to the right, and they made a detour at Yeha, the capital of the ancient D'mat Kingdom. They spent some time visiting the Temple of Yeha and joined a couple of foreign tourists to listen to the history of the ancient civilization from a local guide.

A flawless guide described the fifty-two kings and queens of the D'mat Kingdom that existed before the Kingdom of Aksum. Yared and Tsehay knew everything that the local guide explained, but they attended

as if they didn't know anything. Both knew a lot about Tigrayan history. However, they preferred to shut up and listen on such occasions. When they noticed errors, they asked politely for clarification and tried to convey their opinions without humiliating anyone. At the end of the tour, Tsehay and Yared thanked and complimented the tour guide. They introduced themselves briefly and told him they never met an excellent tour guide like him before.

"Thank you, but I'm not a tour guide. My name is Gebremariam. I was born here, and these are my friends from Canada. I'm just giving them a private tour of my birthplace," he said. They appreciated him even more for the accuracy while he wasn't in the field.

Ezana observed something unusual during their visit to the ancient town of Yeha: "the gateway to the pre-Aksumite civilization," as the native man repeatedly said. The happiness his parents projected had made him think they were going to meet someone special or discover precious treasure, but neither happened.

Ezana heard the guy saying how the Temple of Yeha, known as the "Terrific Temple of the Sun and Moon," was the most ancient structure of the region still standing today and how it was built was still a mystery. However, why his parents were extremely thrilled at that specific attraction remained a mystery for Ezana as the Yeha Temple is for archaeologists.

Ezana took the car key from his dad and walked to the car, contemplating. He pressed the remote on the key to unlocking the vehicle from a distance. The car beeped, and that was when Yared noticed Ezana took the car key from him. Ezana grabbed a bottle of water from the front seat and jumped into the back seat. After spending some quality time alone behind the historical temple of Yeha, Tsehay and Yared marched toward the parked car, hands locked and laughing.

"Where did this sudden euphoria come? Why are you acting like Romeo and Juliet all of a sudden?" Ezana murmured, seeing them coming.

Aksum, their final destination for the day, was only twenty-eight miles away from Yeha. But Adwa, another historical attraction, was waiting for them in the middle.

22

THE FAMILY THAT NEVER KILLS SPIDERS

They drove through the majestic mountains of Adwa to the town of Adwa, and they got the chance to see the mountains close-up.

Fast-forwarding from the ancient history of the D'mat Kingdom to the 19th century of modern history, Tsehay and Yared told Ezana the history of Emperor Yohannes IV, Alula and the battle of Adwa.

Tsehay wrote an essay on the Victory of Adwa back in college. Her main focus on the piece was the role of Bashay Awalom, the double agent spy. When they reached a notable rock, Tsehay told Ezana how Bashay Awalom fooled the Italian army as a double agent and disappeared into thin air after he led them into the Ethiopian army.

"Wow! That's epic, Mom," Ezana shouted, marveled by the story.

When Tsehay perceived Ezana's high level of interest in the story, she wanted to take advantage of the moment and continued telling the story.

"A few weeks before the battle of Adwa, Awalom the spy received a confidential message from General Alula who recruited and used him as a spy in the past. Awalom traveled secretly from Enticho to Adwa.

He met the top leaders of the Ethiopian army in a tent headquarter of Emperor Menelik II. Empress Taytu, the emperor, and his top generals—Alula, Mengesha, Mikael, and Gebeyehu—discussed with Awalom the status of the Italian army.

"Awalom, with a mission to fool the Italians as a double agent, went back to Enticho, near where the Italians were based. Then he approached the Italians' camp and presented to the Italian commanders alluring information cooked by general Alula. The information he provided was too believable, and the Italians agreed to advance and attack at the day and time Awalom proposed. Soon, around twenty thousand soldiers led by five generals marched toward Adwa, singing and shouting in a winning spirit.

"Awalom made sure that the Italian army entered the circle of the Ethiopian patriots. According to the plan, he asked Commander General Oreste Barateiri to let him answer the call of nature, which he did. The general stopped his army and waited until the spy peed and got back to lead them to their predicted victory.

"Awalom had put his Kuta over a rock to send a signal that he was urinating under the rock. The general and his army waited and waited, but Awalom couldn't finish his business and get back. They still could see his Kuta on the rock though. General Barateiri became impatient and ordered soldiers to bring him immediately. Awalom wasn't there.

They found only his Kuta. The soldiers searched the area, but they couldn't find any trace of Awalom. They shouted back to the general and informed him Awalom wasn't there. The news shocked the general. Furiously, the general ordered his soldiers to go after him.

"Awalom accomplished his mission and disappeared into thin air. Because of the intelligence provided and the trick he played, the battle between the Ethiopian and Italian armies took only six hours. The Ethiopian patriots achieved a remarkable victory that inspired the world to end colonization."

Ezana listened, nodding his head. "What happened to Awalom? How did he manage to escape?"

"That's a great question, and there is a fascinating answer for it," Tsehay said. She sipped from her bottled water.

"Awalom had put his Kuta on the rock for camouflage and left the area as fast as he could. When he heard footsteps of soldiers following him, he did his best to run back to Enticho, but he was too old to outrun the young soldiers. When he sat to breathe, he saw some soldiers coming closer with their guns out. He got up and continued running, using his last grams of energy.

"Luckily, he saw fox holes, and one of them was covered by a spider's web. He decided to hide inside the hole with the spider's web. He opened the web with care so that he could put it back as it was once he entered. He managed to do it well. Soon, he heard the soldiers searching everywhere, including the fox holes, but they didn't care to search the one Awalom was in since a spider's web covered it. They thought that was an abandoned fox hole.

"Shortly after, Awalom heard the sound he was expecting: guns and the thundering roar of the Ethiopian patriots. He smiled in relief inside the hole. When the war commenced, the soldiers gave up searching for Awalom and went back to join the battle." Tsehay paused for another sip of water.

"Cool!" Ezana exclaimed.

"And," Tsehay continued, "since a spider's web saved Awalom, his family felt compassion for spiders and stopped hurting them. They embraced them as members of their family. And the compassion for spiders has continued as a legacy in the family for generations even today."

The story blew Ezana's mind. "Oh, man! Too many epic stories all over the place."

Tsehay and Yared nodded in agreement.

23

HIDDEN TREASURES

After Yeha, the attraction both Tsehay and Yared wanted to revisit was Enda Abba Garima Monastery. The monastery housed precious treasures such as the oldest copy of the Holy Bible, The Garima Gospels, and the tomb of Africa's first general, Alula Aba Nega. But neither of them mentioned valuable treasures as the main reason for craving to revisit the monastery. They had a romantic motive in mind.

Yared descended to the historical town of Adwa delicately while Tsehay and Ezana enjoyed looking at the mountains of Soloda and Gesessew on both sides of the road. Yared turned to the left when he entered the town and ascended to the dramatic cliffs that enfolded the ancient historical monastery.

When they finished climbing and reached on top of the hills, the beautiful churches of Abba Garima Monastery revealed from surrounded mountains. Yared and Tsehay looked at each other when they saw the churches. Suddenly, they both lit up like Christmas trees again.

Ezana, amazed by their sudden change, asked them what was unique about the churches. They explained how ancient the monastery was and the precious treasures in its small museum.

They entered the church's compound, and Yared and Tsehay burst into laughter. Ezana shook his head and jumped out of the car.

"King Ezana, welcome to Enda Abba Garima!" Yared said.

A charming young priest welcomed them. The Denver family kissed a hand cross the priest pulled out. He blessed each of them with his cross and gave them time to pray before the visit.

"Abba Garima, one of The Nine Saints who arrived in Aksum in the 5th century to preach Christianity, chose this spectacular place as his sanctuary. Praise the Lord. The Saint blessed us with the sacred gifts of the Garima Gospels," the priest explained to Ezana.

"And translated from Greek to Ge'ez by Abba Garima himself, the Garima Gospels are The World's Oldest Illuminated Manuscripts found in the monastery's museum," Yared said.

"According to tradition, God miraculously stopped the sun in the sky to allow Saint Abba Garima to complete the three remarkable Gospels in a single day," Tsehay added.

"Wow! Cool," Ezana radiated.

Tsehay and Yared came back after fifteen years, and something pleasantly surprised them. The monastery encompassed two churches. One church opened for both sexes, and the other a men's monastery.

The museum and the tomb of General Alula Aba Nega moved to the church where both sexes were welcomed. Tsehay finally got the chance to visit the general's newly built burial chamber outside by a philanthropist, Dawit Gebregziabher.

General Alula's tent with his blood from the last wound that led to his death was displayed in the museum. Ezana never expected to experience the great general's blood close up, and that blew his mind.

"The trip covered General Alula's history highlights from birth to death. Did you guys plan this, or was it just a coincidence?" Ezana asked when they got back in the car and started returning to Adwa.

Even happier, his parents both described that they didn't plan it simultaneously with the same words, which made them explode to laughter.

No matter what your secret reason is, it's awesome to see you both happy again, Ezana said to himself and leaned back in his seat.

Tsehay stopped talking and started scrolling her phone. Yared got the message, and he focused on driving downhill to Adwa.

Ezana heard his stomach growling. He calculated the number of hours since he ate breakfast in Adigrat and a slice of himbasha as a snack in Enticho. He realized his parents were happy enough to forget lunch and perhaps even dinner if he didn't remind them. His stomach rumbled again.

"Sorry, baby. We'll eat lunch shortly," Tsehay said.

"Did you hear that?" Ezana asked.

Tsehay turned around and showed him a pity face with regret. "Yes, I did. Sorry."

"I stopped the music because your stomach is rumbling a lot. A DJ in your stomach took over and played the soundtrack for our road trip," Yared said and burst into laughter.

Tsehay wanted to laugh but held it in when she saw Ezana's straight face. Yared saw both of them, and he cut his laughter short. Suddenly, Ezana started laughing. Tsehay and Yared echoed him.

"You never joked like that, Dad. Good one."

"My sense of humor improves when I am hungry. The problem is I hate to be hungry."

"Nobody likes to be hungry, hun," Tsehay said. "Where can we eat?"

"All food is delicious when you are starving, but I'll ask someone when we reach the center of town," Yared said.

24

HAPPY COINCIDENCE

In the summer, the majestic mountain of Soloda became green and pleasing to the eye. Tsehay took some pictures of the historic town, which extended under the notable mountain.

Yared asked one of the shoeshine boys, his favorite people to ask for information, where to eat. The boy gave him the names and directions of his top three favorite restaurants in the city. Yared tipped the boy and headed to the number one restaurant, according to the shoeshine.

They parked the car on the street and entered the small restaurant. A waitress told them the washroom was in the back.

As always, Tsehay scanned the walls of the restaurant, looking for some paintings. She loved the artwork of local artists they put in small restaurants and cafés. Some artwork made her laugh, and others made her think. The good ones urge her to look for their creators.

She admired the café and restaurant owners in the small towns for their aesthetic. And she mentioned them as a good example when people argued with her, saying, "Spending time and money just to appreciate arts is for the rich."

"Mom, really?" Ezana said, narrowing his eyes on her.

"Ezana loves food more than art," Yared said, jokingly.

Tsehay apologized, and they crossed the main restaurant to the backside, and they found the open backyard more appealing than inside. Another waitress led them to an empty table for four with one extra chair for Tsehay's handbag.

When goats and lambs bleated right behind them, Yared explained it meant fresh food, and they were waiting for their turn to become fresh food.

All three of them were starved and didn't have an appetite to see the menu. Yared walked to one of the busy waitresses to make the order, and he didn't tell Tsehay and Ezana what he ordered. Mouthwatering fried lamb and goat meat were flying over them to other people, which made Ezana's stomach rumble again.

Their waitress came with a large empty tray, and she put it on their table. She went back to the kitchen and came back carrying another big tray holding three plates of food with fresh goat meat, lamb meat, and salad. The carrot, tomato, and lettuce of the salad gave an excellent color to the food. Ezana never saw such a mix, but he liked it and gave two thumbs up after a couple of bites.

While they were working on their food, Tsehay saw someone walking in and nudged Yared on the shoulder to show him. Both stopped eating, dumbfounded. Ezana followed their gaze and saw a nobody to him.

The guy walked to the handwashing sink and stood behind a couple of young men, waiting for his turn. One of the young men saw the guy. He said something to his friends, and they all greeted the guy respectfully and let him wash first.

Yared, mouthful, turned to Tsehay and nodded to confirm that she was right.

"I know," Tsehay said.

From the way his parents acted, Ezana guessed the guy was some kind of VIP and kept watching the scene while eating.

Tsehay gave Yared another push on the shoulder to talk to him. Yared put back a bite he was preparing to eat. He stood and waited for the guy on the way between the tables of the restaurant.

"Fiseha?" Yared asked the guy.

"Yes," the guy said.

"Yared. It's a true honor for my family and myself to meet you," Yared said and invited him to join them.

Fiseha declined the invitation politely. Yared turned to his wife and gave her a signal to help him convince the guy. She introduced herself, where they came from, and how they were huge fans of his brother, the late Prime Minister Meles Zenawi. He noticed how her voice trembled when she mentioned his brother and agreed to join them.

Fiseha looked a lot like his brother. That was why they identified him quickly. His presence and memories of his brother evolved their ordinary lunch into a historic moment. Even Ezana also became excited. He knew how his parents loved Meles Zenawi, and he grew up seeing his photos everywhere in their Denver home.

Touched by the stories he heard, Fiseha offered for them to visit the house where Meles Zenawi was born. They jumped on the chance without a blink and visited the small house that birthed the great leader.

"This is your lucky day," Ezana said while his parents were in complete awe in Meles's study room.

After a quick tour around the house, they discussed the potential of the place for a great museum. They took pictures together, exchanged addresses, and drove off to Aksum.

25

A MATCH MADE IN HEAVEN

During the family vacation, Ezana learned a lot about his parents. They shared similar hobbies, dreams, and passions. They met, fell in love at first sight, and got married because of their shared love for history.

His dad was born and raised in the ancient and historic city of Aksum. Before he moved to America, he had started working as a tourist guide in Aksum right after he graduated from a Hotel and Tourism Institute in Addis Ababa. He never had a plan to leave Aksum, the city he loved. He wanted to live and die there.

Ezana's mom was born in Mekelle but left as a toddler and was raised in the United States of America after her parents fled through Sudan in the early 1990s due to the civil war in Ethiopia. The U.S. government accepted Tsehay and her parents as refugees after they stayed one year at a refugee camp in Sudan. They settled in Denver, Colorado, where Tsehay grew up and went to school.

Tsehay came back to visit her grandma in Mekelle after she graduated from the University of Northern Colorado in African Studies. She met Yared in Aksum, a place that took a great space in her imagination growing up. When they met, both were young and fresh graduates. She was Yared's first client as a tourist on his first day on the job as a self employed tourist guide/driver. She booked him online. He picked her up from Aksum's Emperor Yohannes IV airport.

As she was his first client, his four-wheel-drive vehicle was brand new and spotless. Yared believed in "first impressions" were vital for lasting success. Dressed up in a suit and tie, and he arrived early at the airport and waited for his first tourist with her full name on paper. When the arrivals started coming out, he threw a mint into the air and caught it in his mouth, a game he liked to play. Then he held the name up and above his head and put a broad business smile on his brown face.

Dressed neat, fresh breath, and a broad smile, now I am ready to welcome my first client, Yared thought. He saw a gorgeous young woman pacing toward him, and his business smile transformed into real delight.

"Welcome to the historical city of Aksum," Yared said.

"Thanks. I'm excited to be here," Tsehay replied.

Tsehay showed Yared her pink luggage on the baggage carousel, and he got the luggage and led her out to his parked car. He opened the car door for her and put her bags in the trunk with care. He drove her to the Yeha Hotel, let her checked in, and waited until she freshened up and got ready to start visiting the city.

The first day visiting Aksum was a success. Yared found Tsehay easy to please. His mission, about the first impression thing, worked a lot too. Tsehay was impressed.

During trips between the attractions, they got a chance to know each other. Tsehay was twenty-five, sophisticated, and intelligent for her age with a charming personality and a beauty like Kerry Washington. She drove Yared crazy instantly. He realized love at first sight was far more immeasurable than the first impression.

In the evening of the first day, he took her back to her hotel and went straight to St. Mary of Zion Church. He thanked the Lord, Jesus Christ, and his mother, St. Mary, for the blessings and prayed hard for a happy long-term relationship with her.

When Tsehay got in her hotel room, she dropped her handbag on a coffee table, kicked her trekking shoes off, went to the bathroom, and turned on the faucet to fill the bathtub. She got back into the bedroom, undressed, and went back into the bathroom again. She lay in the tub and reflected on her first day in Aksum. Exploring the traces of the civilization of Aksum was on top of her bucket list. She was in a dream that came true.

Yared was responsible as her guide/driver, and she thought he did a pretty good job. She rated him in every category possible. He knew what to do, what to say, and was in total control of the job. His knowledge about the history of ancient civilizations and his worldview was mind-blowing.

Next, she examined how he made her feel.

My heart didn't pound. My hands didn't shake. My knees didn't go weak, Tsehay thought. *Maybe what the Buddhists say about how you feel when you meet a soulmate is true. You feel calm. No anxiety, and no agitation.*

She melted in thoughts of him. *He's respectful. He lacks a sense of humor, but the way he does things is funny.* She smiled. *Or maybe it's too early to judge his sense of humor.*

On day two, Yared arrived early and waited for Tsehay in the parking lot of the Yeha Hotel. She came out at 8:00 A.M. on time. She saw him throw a mint into the air and catch it in his mouth.

"Impressive!" she said.

"Practice," he said. "You want a mint?"

She accepted his offer and reached out to take one. He refused to give it to her though and said she should earn it. He threw one into the air. She missed catching it. He threw another one. And another one. She grabbed it on the third. Both laughed. That simple act broke the ice, and they became more open to each other.

In no time, they were finishing each other's sentences. They fell in love in the middle of the tour around Tigray. What was more, Yared canceled his plans and drove her to the rest of Tigray.

The extended trip became an opportunity for Tsehay and Yared to get to know each other on a deeper level. They lived in two different worlds but had read similar books. They found out they also had identical passions about history, nature, tourism, and life in general.

In a month, Yared and Tsehay felt like a match made in heaven. At the end of the trip, when Yared drove her to Alula Aba Nega International Airport in Mekelle, they both hated to separate, and tears rolled down their faces.

They lived in the sister cities, Denver, Colorado, and Aksum, Tigray, eight thousand miles away from each other. They kept the flame of their long-distance love alive through romantic emails and phone calls for years until Tsehay married Yared and took him to Denver, Colorado.

Tsehay and Yared didn't tell Ezana yet, but the reason they planned to celebrate his twelfth birthday in Aksum was also to celebrate the fifteen anniversary of their love life. They hoped he would like and consider it as his birthday gift when they revealed to him how, where, and when they met fifteen years back.

Upon the vacation, Ezana observed unusual excitement and happiness in his parents. He also caught them kissing and whispering to each other on some occasions on the trip, but he had no idea they had a secret plan to celebrate something other than his birthday.

26

STRANGE VOICE

After a great lunch and visiting the remarkable birthplace of the late prime minister of Ethiopia in Adwa, driving to Aksum only thirteen miles away was a piece of cake. They arrived while their excitement was still high. Tsehay and Yared beamed even more when they saw the "Welcome to Aksum" sign.

Tsehay turned around to tell Ezana they have arrived, but he was sleepy from overeating Injera. Then Tsehay turned to Yared, but he had vanished into memories since he was born and raised in Aksum. When they passed Emperor Yohannes IV airport gate, Tsehay rewound to the day she met Yared fifteen years ago inside the airport and got lost in their unforgettable, romantic memories.

Yared's parents lived in the city of Aksum, but the family from Denver made a reservation at Yeha Hotel. They preferred to stay in a hotel for convenience reasons. Ezana compromised many things on the trip, including Disneyland, but not a WiFi connection. The Internet was his reward for being considerate of the trip.

On their way to Yeha Hotel, Ezana woke up and saw something through the car window and screamed unconsciously. Yared stopped the car.

"What's that, baby?" Tsehay asked in shock, assuming something happened to her son.

"Look, look!" Ezana pointed his finger.

"You scared the hell out of me!" Tsehay said, inhaling.

"I'm glad you recognize the chapel that housed the most sacred gift God gave to humankind, the Ark of the Covenant," Yared said and continued driving.

"Chapel of the Tablet, of course! We saw it in the Palace of Art we visited in Mekelle," Ezana said.

"I don't think we saw it there...did we?" Yared asked his wife.

"Twice. In the gallery and the prince's private room," Ezana snapped.

"The curator mentioned the church St. Mary of Zion, but we didn't see any painting related to this. You just experienced a deja vu, baby," Tsehay said, smiling at Ezana.

Ezana was about to tell them that he not only saw it twice but also touched it and experienced an electric shock. But he held it back.

The Yeha Hotel had the best view in Aksum, but that wasn't the main reason they wanted to stay in the old hotel instead of the new and fancy ones. Tsehay and Yared wanted to revisit their first meeting and romance. They booked the same room that Tsehay stayed in back then and where they shared unforgettable romantic moments.

The room was pretty much the same after fifteen years. The same paintings hung on the same walls. It would be disappointing if they were ordinary clients of the hotel. But for Tsehay and Yared, the unchanged room helped to bring all the sweet, romantic memories to life.

In the car, Ezana had the chance to scan modern hotels in the streets of Aksum and couldn't figure out why his parents passed all the good-looking hotels and checked into the old Yeha Hotel. And to his surprise, they were unusually thrilled when they entered the old room.

He assumed they wouldn't even notice if he left the room and walked out to let them enjoy their "special moment" that he didn't understand. He crossed a culturally decorated, beautiful glassed restaurant to find a magnificent view. The famous Stelae Field and The Church of St. Mary of Zion, the two prominent landmarks of Aksum, were displayed in front of him.

While he was contemplating and appreciating the attractions, a lovebird flew passed him and landed on a nearby rock. Ezana didn't notice the bird.

"Wow! Maybe this is the reason why they chose this hotel," Ezana whispered to himself.

"Yes, this is the most beautiful view in Aksum," Ezana heard someone say in the sweetest voice he never heard before.

He turned around, but no one was there except the bird. A sweat of fear trickled down his back. Then he rushed back to his parents. He bumped into his mom on her way to look for him. "Hey, we are about to go meet your grandparents. Let's go freshen up," his mom said. She didn't notice his nervousness.

27

MEET THE MONKS

Ezana's grandparents on his dad's side decided to become a nun and a monk and waited for the right time to come. They spent most of their time praying in The Church of St. Mary of Zion as part of their journey to be monastics. When Ezana met his grandparents, they showered him with nonstop kisses and blessings.

Many women were busy around the big house. Yared whispered to Tsehay that they were preparing food and drinks for the next Sunday, the day his parents officially become a nun and a monk.

This house is like a church. Even more church looking than the church we have in Denver, Ezana thought.

A year ago, when Yared's parents decided to become a nun and a monk, their house was redesigned, reconstructed, and decorated by their architect daughter to look and feel like church. Yared, saw the changes for the first time, toured the entire compound but didn't find any trace that could remind him he was born and raised in the same house. The house that Yared could remember had only one eucalyptus tree in the middle of the compound but was now gone and replaced by many indigenous trees.

My sister did a great job, except she also destroyed all my memories, Yared thought.

Yared led Tsehay and Ezana into his room. They entered one by one through a narrow door, stood in the middle, and scanned the room. There was a bed, small bookshelf stuffed with religious books, table, and a chair. Tsehay and Ezana's eyes first looked at the paintings of Jesus Christ, St. Mary, angels, and saints.

"Impressive! Your sister did this too. I mean the artwork?" Tsehay asked, amazed by the beautiful paintings.

"Remember the talented local artists we visited fifteen years ago? She must have commissioned one of them," Yared said, opening the small window.

Tsehay nodded. "This must be the smallest art gallery in the world with so many charming paintings."

"Clean and fresh too. I love it," Ezana added.

"You see, son, this was my room," Yared said. He explained how he spent most of his time studying in the room. Ezana listened while comparing his dad's bedroom with his own back in Denver.

"You hang superhero Hollywood star posters on your walls, and I have paintings of Jesus Christ, Mary, angels, and saints," Yared bragged.

Before Ezana got a chance to respond to his dad, he heard his grandmother's footsteps.

"Dinner is ready," she said.

Ezana's grandma led them into the living room. Friends and neighbors of the family came to welcome the Denver family and to congratulate Ezana's grandparents for their new lives as monastics. Most of them knew Yared, and some of them were his childhood friends. All sat on a cushion of a built-in traditional bench seat that circled the entire living room. All put down their drinks and stood to greet Yared and his family. Yared, Tsehay, and Ezana shook everyone's hands.

Dinner was served following prayers. Ezana wanted to go back to the hotel to be alone and to think about the voice he heard earlier. He couldn't stop thinking about it, though he wanted to be present and focused on his charming grandparents.

And a few minutes later, a story he never expected calmed his urge to leave his grandparents' house. His grandparents decided to become monastic when Ezana turned eleven. He heard his parents talking about it back then but didn't understand it or didn't care. But when Ezana saw both of his grandparents dressed up in their new yellow religious clothing and their broad smiles, he ached to know about them and their new lives as a nun and a monk.

They couldn't speak English, Ezana guessed, and he could only hear and speak a little Tigrigna himself. He wanted to use one of his parents to bridge the gap as a translator, but Yared's old buddy and the invited neighbors engaged them both. *Now I wish I had a superpower for language skills*, Ezana thought. Usually, when someone asked him, "What kind of superpower would you like to have?" his answer was simple, "To be invisible."

He pulled out his phone and typed, "How people become nuns and monks?" The Internet connection took ages to get him answers. While Ezana was looking down at his iPhone, begging for the info, he felt a soft touch on his shoulder. He looked up and saw small sparkling eyes looking down at him. His grandpa, sat next to him.

"What is the matter, son?" Grandpa asked him with a heavy English accent, which surprised Ezana.

"Nothing, Grandpa, but I didn't know..."

"That I can speak English?"

"Yes," Ezana nodded.

"I always like the reaction when I do speak the language."

His grandpa grinned and explained to Ezana how he grew up running after tourists around The Church of St. Mary of Zion and the Obelisks like many kids did in Aksum. He continued describing how working as a local tourist guide helped him learn the language, get a Swiss sponsor for his education, and later get hired by the church.

Ezana was so fascinated that he forgot about the strange voice. His grandpa spoke slowly and over pronounced every word, but his English was quite good.

After he told him his story briefly, Ezana moved to ask the question his curious mind nagged him with the whole evening. "What happened when you and grandma officially become a nun and a monk?"

His grandpa tried to explain the monastic life as much as he could. When he lacked words, he asked Tsehay to help. Ezana shot his final question.

"Why did you want to go into the monastic life?"

His grandpa looked around to check if anyone was watching, leaned toward Ezana, and whispered, "Okay, I am going to tell you, but promise me to keep it to yourself."

"I promise," Ezana whispered back and leaned forward, eager to hear the secret.

"Glory to God," his grandpa said, face glowing. "It's because of you, son." Ezana jerked back.

"It's a great thing. We are blessed to have you," his grandpa said, his face still glowing. "You see, son. Your grandma and I were praying for God to bless us with grandchildren. And we vowed to God that we would become a nun and a monk when we saw a grandchild."

Ezana's jaw dropped, and he kept listening to a story that he never expected would involve him.

"Last year, your father told us he would bring you to us this summer, and we started preparing. Now you are here. God fulfilled our wish. And according to our oath to God, now it's time to enter the monastic life," his grandpa said, beaming like the sun.

"Wow. I don't know what to say, Grandpa," Ezana said. "I mean, I didn't know my existence had this much meaning to anyone."

The story blew Ezana's mind. His mind drifted away to what happened earlier at the hotel. *The voice and now this,* he thought.

"Ezana, you are the greatest gift from God, and to be a nun or a monk means to be closer to God. It's a blessing. We'll pray for you, for your parents, and for the world," his grandpa said, enunciating the words.

Tsehay read the extraordinary situation on Ezana's face and excused herself from the conversation she was having with her husband's old friends.

"How are you two getting along?" she asked.

The grandpa smiled at Tsehay and looked at Ezana to hear his say.

"Grandpa just told me an amazing story I won't forget for the rest of my life," Ezana said.

"Really? What story?" Tsehay asked.

Ezana looked at his grandpa, and he gave him the shush sign by putting his index finger on his lips.

"Sorry, Mom. It's super-secret."

"My question is answered. You two are getting along so well." She went back to her seat.

A great dinner and a few drinks later, friends and neighbors started leaving in ones, twos, and threes. Eventually, only Yared's parents and family remained. The grandparents explained the upcoming church ceremony that marked the beginning of their monastic life.

28

WHAT'S THE STORY OF THE BOY?

At the Yeha Hotel, Ezana paced back and forth outside in front of the most beautiful view in Aksum. He nervously waited for a clue about the strange voice. A group of tourists from different countries, who were enjoying their Aksumite dinner with Aksumit wine inside the all-glassed restaurant, noticed Ezana outside in the dark.

Ezana showed up when the tourists had talked about pretty much everything. But the last bottle of wine ordered by the Brazilian couple was still full. Then they started speculating about Ezana, which later turned into a fun game called, "What's the Story of the Boy Outside?"

They quickly created rules for the game, each one to come up with their theories and, in the end, ask the boy for his real story and see if it matched their assumptions.

"He's the son of this hotel's owner. We think the boy lives in Mekelle city, and he's here for summer vacation," a British couple said.

"I think the boy is from here, but his father, who was originally from here, lives abroad. Now, the father is in town to visit his son. The boy is waiting for his father," archaeology student from Germany guessed.

"I guess the boy came from abroad with his mother to meet his father for the first time. That's why he's nervous," a Sudanese journalist said.

"His mom works here in the hotel. Maybe she's a chef or a receptionist. He is eager to go somewhere, and he's impatiently waiting until she finishes work," said a tourist from Spain.

"I presume from the way he dressed up that the boy came from the United States or Canada. The Internet is slow. He's bored sitting in his room, and that's why he's out there," a Canadian tourist said.

"The boy lives here in Aksum. His close family is staying in the hotel. He came to see them or give them a message, but he didn't find them. He waited and waited. The person he is looking for didn't show up. He didn't expect to stay this late, and that's why he's panicking," the Brazilian couple guessed.

The guessing game about Ezana's story reignited the tourists' table. They ordered another round of drinks. While anticipating the story to unfold, everybody in the group kept trying to convince their logic was better than the others.

An elegant woman entered the restaurant and stole their attention. Suddenly, everyone stopped talking and stared at the beautiful woman—Tsehay—who wandered her eyes across the all-glass restaurant. Tsehay saw Ezana appreciating the view.

She took a seat in a corner of the restaurant to let him enjoy the fresh air outside. The tourists monitored her movement while running their theories in their heads to connect with her. Those who had a better chance to win grinned.

Tsehay glanced at the tourists, smiled casually at them, and went out toward Ezana. All the tourists' eyes followed Tsehay outside. She held the boy from behind and kissed him on both cheeks. From the glass restaurant, the tourists kept watching every move. They saw the boy turn around to Tsehay and explain something to her. The spectators could see but couldn't hear what the boy and the lady talked about. Therefore, they had to connect with their assumptions based on the body language. Some of them even felt they guessed accurately and shouted, "Yes!" as winners.

But then a gentleman in pajamas crossed the restaurant, joined the lady and the boy, and changed the scenario. The scene became more interesting. The tourists paid their undivided attention to the trio. The gentleman put his right hand around the boy's shoulder and squeezed him adorably. The boy used similar gestures he used with the lady to explain something to the gentleman. Again, based on the body language, the tourists tried to match their theories, and some of them cheered.

Tsehay, Yared, and Ezana stood a bit longer, chatting and enjoying the moon and fresh night air until Tsehay mentioned she needed to be back in the room to do some stuff.

The tourists, who were watching the family as actors performing on a stage, adjusted their sitting positions when they saw the trio coming toward them. The Sudanese volunteered to stop the trio and ask them when they passed through the restaurant.

"Excuse me. Do you mind if we ask you a question?"

The three of them stopped without hesitation and smiled at the group.

"Not at all. Please," Tsehay said, and Yared nodded, both still grinning.

The Sudanese explained the funny game they were playing. Tsehay, Yared, and Ezana found it interesting and laughed.

"It's a pretty awesome game," Ezana said.

"Very," Yared said.

"Unfortunately, most of you are going to lose," Tsehay said, giggling. "But what happens to the winner if there is one?"

"The one who guessed the most unlike the actual story pays the bill," the Sudanese said.

Yared, Tsehay, and Ezana quickly scanned the things on the table.

"Wow! It won't be fun for the loser," Yared said and chuckled.

Tsehay told the story of her family briefly, then she said, "Bonne nuit," to all and left with Ezana. Yared stayed behind to play the role of judge of the fun contest and for a beer.

After carefully reviewing all the theories, Yared announced the only one resembling Ezana's real story was the one presumed by the Canadian tourist. All cheered the winner and prepared to split the bill among the rest of them.

But Yared insisted and explained the Tigrayan tradition of karma for treating guests with honor and kindness. He paid for all the drinks, and they thanked him for it.

29

THE FIRST ENCOUNTER WITH A
TALKING BIRD

I t was late when they got back to the hotel room, but Ezana couldn't sleep. He kept staring at the ceiling and thinking. He imagined going to the most beautiful view in town first thing in the morning and trying to find out about the voice.

He woke up early. His parents were still asleep, and he walked out to the most beautiful view in Aksum. He stretched his body, inhaled the fresh morning air, and sat on a chair facing the Stelae Park and The Church of St. Mary of Zion. The lovebird was there before him, but he didn't notice her presence again, which pissed the bird a little bit. She waited until he got relaxed.

"Good morning, Ezana," she said in a soft and sweet voice. Ezan startled, jumped up, and turned 360 degrees to see where the voice came.

"Don't freak out. I am here. It's me, the bird."

He finally saw the little bird and got even more scared. He sprinted like an Olympic athlete in a 100-meter dash and ran back to his room. He jumped into his bed and covered himself beneath a sheet and blanket so that his parents couldn't find out how scared he was. Besides, he knew they would never believe that a bird talked to him twice.

After breakfast, the family went out to visit Aksum. Yared, the former tour guide, was so excited to give an exclusive tour of his hometown to his family. Tsehay loved the way he guided, and that was the main reason she fell in love with him in the first place.

Yared started the tour from the ruined palace of Queen Saba. Then the Chapel of the Tablet, which won Ezana's attention away from thinking about the talking bird. The fact that the great gift of God to humankind, the Ark of the Covenant, was secretly kept in Aksum had always amazed Ezana a lot. His interest multiplied after he experienced the electrical shock from the artwork of the chapel in Palace of Art. His parents were dead sure Ezana didn't see a painting of the chapel, so they didn't bring it up.

Ezana stayed behind at the Chapel of the Tablet, closed his eyes, and hesitantly put his hand on the wall as he did with the painting, expecting the same experience of the electrical shock, but nothing happened.

"Maybe they are right. It was deja vu or just the imagination of my mind like the talking bird," Ezana said jokingly to himself.

"Catch up, baby!" his mom shouted.

They continued their visit inside The Church of St. Mary of Zion and the museum inside the church, then the Stelae field, and another museum behind the Stelae field. Yared enjoyed guiding his family through thousands of years in history. Ezana, again preoccupied with thoughts of the talking bird, missed some of the incredible explanations Yared gave. Tsehay observed Ezana's inattention and suggested to continue visiting the rest of the attractions after lunch.

After the lunch break, Ezana told his parents he wasn't feeling okay and wanted to rest. They urged him to see a doctor if he was not well. Otherwise, he shouldn't miss the afternoon shift because they wanted him to see King Ezana's inscriptions.

"I'm not feeling like going either. Please let me stay in the room," Ezana said, begging.

They had no choice but to postpone the tour for the next day. Ezana stayed in bed until his parents went out for coffee, and then he walked out to the most beautiful view in Aksum to face the bird.

Few tourists were on the spot enjoying the view and drinks. He scanned the whole area, but the bird wasn't there. He passed through the tourists to the rock where he saw the bird in the morning. He waited and waited, but the talking bird didn't show up.

Maybe there wasn't a talking bird. Maybe I created it in my imagination, Ezana thought and started walking back to his room.

"Ezana, I'm here. Come back," said the lovebird.

Ezana stopped walking, but he wasn't sure if the bird was real or just in his head.

"I'm real. Please follow me," the bird continued.

Ezana turned and followed the bird without thinking. The bird landed on a nearby rock. Ezana walked toward her and hesitated on what to do next.

"Ezana, I know this is a strange experience for you. And I know your name, and that takes the weirdness to another level. It's too much for you, but trust me, it's going to be an awesome experience. Welcome to the holy city," the bird said.

Feeling surreal and impressed at the same time, Ezana sat next to the bird. She waited for him to say something, but he kept mute.

"I expected you to have millions of questions for me," the bird said, giggling and waving her wings in a sense of encouragement.

"I do, but I'm not sure if this is a dream or really happening," Ezana answered in a low voice and looked around to check if people were paying attention.

"Fair enough. I understand this is an unusual situation. But believe me, you're going to love it. Go back to your room and rest. See you around. Bye for now." The bird flew away.

Ezana regretted the missed opportunity of talking with the bird instantly. He walked into his hotel room, thinking, Dear God, if this is a dream, please don't wake me up until I speak with the bird.

In his room, Ezana couldn't do anything, not even reading his favorite comic books or watching the superhero movies he adored. He decided to try again before his parents came back from the city.

He went out to the same spot, hoping the bird would come back, and he sat on a rock next to the rock the bird sat on. Before long, he heard the bird calling his name while landing on her spot. Ezana jarred when she called his name as if he didn't expect her.

"I'm glad you came," she said.

"Thanks, bird."

"So, your birthday is around the corner. Is there a party, and am I invited?" the bird asked.

Ezana was about to explode when he heard that.

"Get over it, Ezana. I'm not an ordinary bird. I know a lot about you." She giggled and waved her wings in excitement.

"It's too much to handle. First, you are a talking bird, and now, you know everything. I don't even know if this is a dream or real," Ezana said.

"As I said, I'm a special bird with lots of spiritual wisdom from God. That's how I know everything about you and everybody. Any questions?" the bird asked, smiling.

"I have millions."

"Okay, I am listening," the bird comforted herself to take his questions.

"Ummm...how long have you been here? My parents know a lot about this place, but they never mentioned you."

"Well, I have been around for a long time, but I show myself only to the chosen. You are one of them," the bird said. "Congratulations, by the way."

"Thanks. But how and why am I chosen?"

"Great question, Ezana, but I don't have an answer for that. Only God knows that."

Ezana was confused. The bird told him a few seconds ago that she was a unique bird who knew everything about everyone, but now, she said she doesn't know.

"I know what you are thinking. And you are right, but only God knows that information. You can ask God why He chose you for this."

When the bird knew what he was thinking, Ezana stopped thinking and froze. After he came back to his senses, he decided to ask her straight instead of contemplating inside his head.

"How can I ask God?" he said sheepishly.

"By going there and praying." The bird pointed her one wing toward The Church of St. Mary of Zion. "But that's not the most important thing here. The most important thing is that God has chosen you. You are blessed. So, rather than asking why, you should be grateful and thank God for it."

Ezana's face beamed and stared at the church in front of him, speechless. The bird stayed quite too.

"Another question, how did you learn to speak English like this?"

The bird beamed her turn with delight. "I can answer this question in many languages of the world, and the answer is I didn't learn it. God gave me the ability to speak in different languages. I don't even know how many languages I can speak." The bird paused as if counting numbers of the languages she could speak.

Ezana, fascinated about everything she said, asked her to tell him more about herself. She revealed to him that she was from the lovebird species, and her family had a long history of serving God and humankind. She also proudly stated how her ancestors helped St. Yared when he composed his sacred music. She then told him how Aksum was a holy place and blessed with so much of God's grace.

"My last question for today...how old are you?" Ezana asked.

"Another great question, Ezana. We are called lovebirds because of our commitment to our love life. We fall in love with our soulmates, and we stay devoted to each other. When one of us dies, the other doesn't survive. I was supposed to die many centuries ago when my husband died, but God gave me tremendous wisdom and saved me to be around to tell stories and his miracles. To answer your question, I don't know exactly how old I am. I stopped counting many, many years ago."

"You are turning twelve in a few days, am I right?"

Ezana was about to get shocked when she mentioned his exact age, but he remembered what she said and that she knew a lot more.

"Yes. It's a big deal for kids like me. I was supposed to celebrate my birthday at Disneyland in the US. You know where that is, right?" he asked the bird, hesitating.

"In the United States of America, I know. Now stop the pity party, and let's plan a happy party for your birthday," the bird said passionately.

The lovebird broke the news to him that there would be a surprise plan for his birthday. Ezana was thrilled and became curious to know what, where, and when, but the bird said, "Surprise is a surprise."

***

That late afternoon, Ezana was so excited like never before. His parents were glad to see his great mood. Both wanted so badly to know the reason behind his happy attitude and annoyed him with questions.

"Okay, I'll tell you the reason, but I want you to promise me something," Ezana said.

Both parents nodded their heads.

"I'll tell you the general reason, but I don't want you to ask me for details."

"Deal!" Tsehay said, and Yared nodded, agreeing with her.

"Grandpa told me a secret yesterday."

"Okay, and the secret is?" Yared asked.

"We call it a secret because we don't tell it. And don't forget you promised not to ask questions."

"But baby, you are super happy today, this afternoon to be exact, not yesterday," Tsehay said, puzzled.

"Aha!" Yared said, satisfied by his wife's question.

"Yes, he told me yesterday, but it left me dumbfounded. I did some reflections alone this afternoon, and I found the thing Grandpa told me is rather delightful." He walked to his room.

Ezana joined his parents with a great sense of enthusiasm to continue visiting the rest of the attractions in Aksum. He asked many questions during the tour, which his parents liked to answer. When unsatisfied with some of their answers, Ezana smiled and made notes in his head to ask his new friend, the lovebird.

At dinner, his parents announced the itinerary for the next couple of days, which was driving to Shire Endasilassie to visit family and the ancient town discovered by archeologists at Mai-Adrasha. Then they would continue to Kafta Sheraro National Park and spend a night in the city of Humera with a family friend who moved there from Denver and started a hotel and sesame exporting business.

Ezana didn't see that coming. He thought they were ending their trip at Aksum and going back to Mekelle after his birthday. He wanted to spend more time with his new friend, the bird. The plan made him crave the bird even more. He looked at the bird's spot through the glassed wall of the Yeha Hotel restaurant.

His parents expected him to love their next stop at the national park since they knew he liked animals, but he didn't react as they expected him to. Ezana kept twirling spaghetti with his fork and looking through the glass without putting any into his mouth.

"So, what do you say, baby?" Tsehay asked.

"You must be excited. You know, we could see elephants, lions, and ostriches among many animals at the Kafta Sheraro National Park," Yared said.

The lovebird flew across the restaurant. Ezana saw her landing at her spot through the all-glass restaurant. Suddenly, he beamed. He thought that was a sign.

"I'd like to stay here. You can go without me," Ezana said.

"You know we can't leave you here alone. That's impossible," Tsehay said firmly.

"Right. That's out of the question," Yared added.

"Who said I was staying alone?" Ezana asked.

Both put down their forks eagerly to hear what he was proposing.

"I'll stay with my grandparents."

Tsehay and Yared's jaws dropped. They looked at each other and then stared back at Ezana as if to say, "What about the Internet?"

They thought he was addicted to the Internet and wouldn't survive without it. They demanded further explanations for his decision to stay behind with his grandparents. Ezana reminded them about the secret he shared with his grandpa.

"The secret is the secret for my decision to stay with them," he said.

Tsehay and Yared didn't expect that and tried to convince him to go with them, but he insisted on staying. It was difficult for them to accept the idea right away, but finally, they did.

30

A MAGIC DOOR TO THE PAST

Early in the morning, a bell boy moved their luggage after Yared asked the hotel manager to store their stuff for a couple of days. Three of them ate breakfast together at the hotel.

Tsehay and Yared warned Ezana with dos and don'ts while staying with his grandparents. Happy Ezana listened, nodding his head.

His parents stuffed their essentials for two days in a small bag, dropped Ezana off at his grandparents', and set off their road trip to Shire Enda Selassie, Sheraro, and Humera.

Ezana's grandparents were so pleased when they heard the news the previous day and smiled sunnily when Ezana walked in with his backpack. But as happy as his grandparents were, they didn't want him to be bored during the daytime, so they planned to take him to a family friend's house where Ezana could play with boys and girls his age.

Both dressed in full yellow fabric, his grandparents sat in front of him gleaming, and his grandpa, with his exciting accent, described what they planned for him. Ezana thanked them for their thoughtfulness, and he let them know what he planned to do.

In the mornings, he walked with them to The Church of St. Mary of Zion and prayed with them. Then he climbed to Yeha Hotel, pretending to read his comic book. His decision made the lovebird happy, and she wanted him not to regret his decision. She asked him what his dream birthday gift would be.

"Going to Disneyland and watching my favorite movie characters come to life," Ezana answered.

"You love movies?" the bird asked.

"More than anything else," Ezana replied.

"Have you watched Night at the Museum?"

Ezana was about to faint again when the bird mentioned the movie.

"Ezana, I am trying to be modest here. I know you would freak out if I speak my mind," the bird said.

Ezana composed himself. "Yes, I watched three of them," he replied, trying to hide his amazement.

"You must like the story if you watched three of them."

"Absolutely!" Ezana answered.

"Awesome. Now let's walk," the bird said and jumped on Ezana's shoulder.

She directed him toward The Church of St. Mary of Zion. While walking down the street, the bird amused Ezana by talking about fairy tale movies and Disneyland in detail. She told him to stop at a specific location.

"I'm trying hard to impress you by using cool words like kids your age use, but you didn't even notice," the bird pretended to be pissed.

"No, no, no! Please don't feel bad. I appreciated all that. But compared to the amazing things you are capable of and the miracle stuff happening right now, you know... " Ezana came up short of the right words to convince the bird.

The bird patted his back and nodded. "I know it's hard to process," she said. "I want you to come right here tonight at midnight."

Ezana waited for the bird to say more, but she didn't. "What for?" Ezana asked.

"You like fairy tales, but God wants to take your desires to another level. I'll be your honorable tour guide to your special visit." The bird flew away without waiting for his response.

Ezana joined his grandparents at the church. They prayed together and went home. Ezana studied the way to his grandparents' house from the meeting location with the bird. He ate his dinner. His grandma let him talk to his parents on the phone. He chatted with them, and they sounded to him like they were on their honeymoon. There wasn't Internet or TV in the house, so Ezana prayed with his grandparents instead.

He set the alarm for 11:45 P.M. and went to bed early. He was so excited that he couldn't sleep, and he got up before the alarm went off. He made it to the meeting place five minutes early. The bird was already there waiting for him.

"Ezana, why didn't you sleep?" the bird asked.

Ezana gave her a look and shook his head as if to say, "Unbelievable."

"I was afraid you might fall asleep, you know," the bird explained.

"But how? How did you do that?" Ezana asked.

"Come on. I know everything under the sun. So, are you ready for the most amazing experience of your life?"

"That's why I didn't sleep," Ezana answered, beaming in delight like a kid in a candy shop.

The lovebird jumped onto his shoulder, and suddenly, a ray of light prevailed over a pathway. She lit the way she wanted him to walk through. He studied the beam of light coming out of her eyes.

"Enough with the wondering look. Let's go before it's too late to catch the time machine," the bird said.

"A time machine? Cool!" Ezana shouted.

They walked up toward the swimming pool of Queen Saba with the guide of the bird's light. When they passed the swimming pool and started to climb to the Tombs of King Kaleb and Gebremeskel, Ezana recognized the places.

"I came here yesterday, you know," he said.

The bird nodded and signaled him to keep walking.

"I have many questions about the time machine you mentioned, but I think you are not in the mood for talking," Ezana said with a trembling voice.

"Why is your voice shaking? Are you afraid?"

"I have never been out here this late. I have never met a bird that can talk and create a ray of light. Yes, I am freaking afraid."

The bird laughed out loud. Ezana looked around to make sure no one heard the bird's loud laughter.

"Don't worry. As long as I touched you, you are invisible. Nobody can see, hear, or smell you. Relax," the bird said and continued laughing.

"Wow! Really? This is a dream came true. I always wanted to have a superpower to become invisible." Ezana joined the laughter out of both nervousness and happiness.

When they arrived at the Tombs of the Kings, the lovebird led him with her light to enter into the Tomb of King Kaleb. Ezana walked down the stairs made of large pieces of stones. When stepping down, he started feeling something strange like a blissful sensation. He continued stepping down into the tunnel made of extra-large rocks until the bird told him to stop. He reached a dead-end, and the bird told him to sit and wait. Ezana sat excited, but he didn't know what to expect.

"You'll see the miracle at 1:00 A.M, which is in seven minutes," said the bird, looking at the enormous one-piece stone wall. Ezana checked his watch. The bird was correct about the time without any clock. *Stop wondering and go with the flow of the miracle,* Ezana said to himself.

Precisely at 1:00 A.M, something glittering appeared at the large rock wall.

"It's time," the bird announced and touched the glittering button that looked like a high-tech touch gate entrance to Elon Musk's secret room.

A secret door opened and unveiled a bright room with a large safe box. The bird flew toward the big box and maneuvered forward and backward like a hummingbird to unlock it. A sophisticated time machine appeared.

The bird asked Ezana to look at the time machine menu and select his favorite period in the history of the Aksumite Kingdom. Ezana was blown away about everything happening. He stood stunned in front of the time machine without knowing what to select. The bird helped him by explaining some of the exciting periods.

"Since your name is Ezana, you might be interested in this one," said the bird as she pointed at the topic of 'King Ezana of Aksum' on the menu.

What Yohannes said to him, echoed in his head, "With great names like yours and mine comes great inspirations."

Ezana clicked 'King Ezana of Aksum.' Then to his surprise, many options with short video trailers popped up. The sub-topic 'King Ezana's Gold Coins' showed when King Ezana's gold coins were being minted from melting gold. A video trailer called 'King Ezana and His Military Campaigns' showed when King Ezana successfully conquered Meroe, the capital city of the Kingdom of Kush in present-day Sudan. Ezana noticed another intriguing video trailer titled 'King Ezana and Christianity' and he clicked on it without thinking.

The time machine box locked. A small vehicle that looked like a bobsled rolled down from the high ceiling of the deluxe room with two comfortable seats. The lovebird jumped into the sled chair and signaled Ezana to follow her lead. He climbed in, and the automatic seat belts fastened them in. A gate on one side of the giant wall opened, and a blinding bright floodlight came in and lit up the room. Ezana covered his eyes. He thought he lost his sight until the sled flew, vanished, and landed in the heart of a 4th-century kingdom.

"Welcome to the 4th-century of Aksum," the lovebird said right after they touched down on a dramatic, breathtaking landscape with towering mountains and lush green fields and forest.

"How is this...wow..." Ezana started talking but halted himself when he saw caravans, elephants, and people passing by.

"Go ahead. We are invisible. We are protected from all the human senses," the lovebird said.

"Really? That's awesome!"

"I know. And you were saying?"

"We just hopped into that vehicle in the dark, and in a few minutes, boom! We're thousands of years back. In daylight. How is this possible?"

"I recommend that you read Mathew 19:26 in the Holy Bible," the lovebird said. "Now, let's walk through some historical events, shall we?"

She landed on Ezana's shoulder, and he followed the people and their exotic animals. Ezana walked wordlessly but examined everything around him. He observed the enormous difference of the thousands of years in between the world he came from and the one he was miraculously visiting. The clothes of the people reminded him of people in the movies about the history of Jesus Christ he watched during Christmas. The topography of the area, the pleasing aroma of the plants and the fresh smell of the air, the way the people walked and talked, everything was hard for him to link up with his own world.

He realized they landed on the skirts of the city of Aksum when they approached a massive entrance. People and animals of diverse shapes and sizes flooded toward the Aksumite gates from different directions. Soldiers stood and controlled the flow.

"You are lucky. Today is a market day," the bird said.

"Oh! That's why the crowd is flowing." Ezana nodded. "By the way, what year is it now?"

"Great question. We are in the year 316."

"And who is the king? Ezana?"

"You'll see," the lovebird answered. "I want to drink water before we enter the city. Follow me."

She flew off his shoulder to the left toward a jungle of big trees. He followed her. When he got closer to the forest, the sound waves of beautiful music composed by nature flowed through his body. Birds were singing and chirping, and a river stream burbled as it traveled through the jungle. On top of the incredible sounds Ezana enjoyed listening to and the beauty he liked seeing, the pleasing smell was more aromatic than a fragrance store at the 16th Street Mall in Denver.

Ezana closed his eyes while listening to the music and inhaled the aroma of the fresh air. "Wow! What a paradise."

The lovebird sipped some water from the flowing river. "Are you listening to the music my family is making?"

"Yes. It's amazing."

"Help yourself," the lovebird said. "It's clean and fresh." She threw her mouth into the river again.

Ezana knelt down by the bank of the river and surveyed the water. It was so clean that he could see multicolored pebbles in the bed. He dove his mouth in and drank lots of water. In the heavenly jungle, the sweet smell and fantastic music of nature carried them away and almost made Ezana forget where they were and why. He kept walking on the edge of the river, and the lovebird flew behind.

Suddenly, a loud scream of women startled them. Ezana ducked down. He couldn't see the lovebird, and he heard his heart pounding. The scream was replaced by yelling and then talking.

"I saw a stranger," a woman said.

"I saw an alien boy," another woman cried.

Ezana crawled in the tall grasses and scanned the river. He saw the women putting their clothes on. And he felt a vibration on the ground. Something was running toward him.

"Bird, where are you?" he whispered desperately.

The vibration increased, and he heard some feet striking the ground. Ezana crawled in the jungle. The lovebird landed on his shoulder, which made him jump and scream loud. She burst into her peculiar laughter. Her laughter calmed him, but he didn't enjoy it this time.

A group of men nearby rushed to help when they heard the screaming women who were taking bath in the river. They just passed in front of him to hunt the alien the women saw. Ezana put his hand on the lovebird's mouth to shush her. And three wet beautiful women followed the men, trying to convince them of what they saw.

"What was that?" Ezana asked the lovebird, terrified.

"I was up in the tree looking at your reactions. It was epic," The lovebird said, still laughing.

"It's not funny. I could have died out of the shock," Ezana said painfully.

The lovebird ceased laughing. "The women saw you. Every time you drink or eat, you become visible, and you remained so unless you touch me, or I touch you."

He nodded and remained silent in bewilderment.

"I didn't plan that, but it was amazing to watch." She continued laughing.

A boy from the 21st century dressed in *Nike* shoes, sportswear, and a baseball cap just happened to be in a 4th-century jungle? Ezana pondered. *They are absolutely right to say they saw an alien. I would freak out too.*

31

WALKING THROUGH AN ANCIENT MARKET

E zana and the lovebird reached the entrance to the 4th-century city of Aksum. Ezana was intimidated by the armed and well built soldiers, and he stood in front of them, confused. The lovebird reminded him again that he was invisible. He smiled and passed through the giant guards and massive gates made of rocks.

Beyond the entrance, receiving directions from the lovebird, Ezana kept walking down a busy cobblestoned street. Although the road was busy with people, animals, and carts, Ezana and the lovebird walked comfortably, untouched, unseen, and unheard. Down the busy road, Ezana heard loud noises from afar. A big open market unfolded in front of them. People were buying and selling animals. Some of them shouted prices to attract buyers. The diverse ancient animal market fascinated Ezana. He stopped to look at the transactions.

"Let's go. We have so much to see," the lovebird said.

Ezana continued walking on the 4th-century road among the people of the ancient kingdom. They reached a market of grains, vegetables, and fruits, and he noticed people bargaining for many unfamiliar fruits and vegetables.

"Interesting!" Ezana said.

"I know," the lovebird replied.

Ezana strode faster. The lovebird told him to turn right on a curve, and a colorful roadside market that seized his attention appeared. The people on this side of the market were fewer, calmer, and more stylish than the people they saw in the other markets. Handcrafts, ivory, jewelry, Chinese silk clothes, Persian carpets, and curtains graced the roadside market. And women dominated both as buyers and sellers, Ezana observed. This side of the market was intriguing. Ezana had to walk slowly.

"Now to the right," the lovebird said.

Ezana did and sensed a smell that he had experienced before. The more he walked ahead, the more robust the scent became. When passed by the incense market, he recalled that his mom liked to put some incense on fire when she made traditional coffee. Ezana realized that the sense of smell was so powerful. That little smell of incense took him thousands of years back from the 4th to the 21st century and thousands of miles from Aksum to Denver.

At the end of the street, there was a giant tree with a big, circled shade, and many people were under the tree watching something. Ezana used the privilege of his invisibility to penetrate. To the delight of the spectators, different magicians were performing their acts. A magician presented a fire-eating performance, and the crowd applauded and cheered him. Another magician came out with a huge python. Ezana froze, sweat started rolling down his back, and then he ran away like a lunatic. The lovebird almost died laughing out loud.

"I'm afraid of snakes," Ezana said after he calmed himself.

And then there were guys calling out loud pedestrians. Ezana asked the bird what their business was.

The lovebird explained about the famous astrologists. "They can delay or hurry plans such as traveling and wedding by predicting the future," the lovebird added.

"It's incredible how the ancient wasn't how I pictured it," Ezana said.

"Aksum had many intellectuals, including philosophers, linguists, and astronomers. If you are lucky, you will see them in action in some of the periods we are going to visit," the lovebird said proudly.

"Awesome," Ezana beamed.

When they arrived in the vicinity of the palace, Ezana noticed Arabs, Whites, and Orientals. He also heard different languages, and to his surprise, he understood all of them.

"Hey, bird," Ezana whispered. "I think I'm listening to different languages, some of them foreign to me."

"You are in one of the most civilized empires in the world. Many merchants, magicians, philosophers, miners, builders, and artisans come from all over the world," the lovebird said.

"And I understand all the languages. How?" Ezana asked, astonished.

"Again, Mathew 19:26." the lovebird answered.

32

WHITE SLAVES

The last street that took them to the palace of the Aksumite Kingdom ended up at one of the entrances of the castle. The broad road with pedestrian sidewalks ran under tall palm trees and flowers on both sides. A few stylish people walked, and others rode elephants or horse carts on the polished cobblestone to and from the palace.

"This road looks like a road to a paradise," Ezana said.

"Yes. The kingdom gives special attention to aesthetic pleasure," the lovebird replied.

Outside of the graceful gate of the tall walled palace stood armed soldiers. More soldiers were watching people going in and out from towers around the walls. Ezana started feeling anxious when he got closer to the entrance, and the lovebird reminded him that he was an invisible kid from the future. That reminder helped him to walk in tall.

The entrance they chose had a panoramic view of the entire palace, and the view was mind-blowing. To Ezana's surprise, the landscaping, the statues, the ornaments, the buildings, and the varieties of animals he saw in a field were beyond his imagination and expectation. He looked around with his mouth and eyes wide open.

The lovebird gave Ezana a moment to appreciate the extraordinary beauty beyond the walls. The cobblestoned road that brought them from outside went straight and connected the main chamber of the palace with the outer world. Other smaller paths met with it from different gates. Ezana kept surveying the details to the left and right of the main road. Machu Picchu looked like buildings, statues, vegetation, towering trees, flowers, a playground, and animals in the fields of both sides.

"Good. Finally, your jaws are back. We have a long history to cover in a day. Now, let's climb up those steps and see what's down there," the lovebird said.

Ezana did as she said, and another playground unveiled. Smaller in size but beautifully designed and developed as an amphitheater for a limited audience.

"The difference between the Aksum we are in and the Aksum we came from is incredible. Where did all of this go?" Ezana asked.

"As the scientists say, most of this we see here in the old Aksum is buried under the present-day Aksum," the lovebird replied.

I must discuss this with Uncle John. He said he is an archaeologist, Ezana thought.

"Let's start watching a scene that leads us to more of a long history," the lovebird said, jumping off Ezana's shoulder. Ezana sat next to the bird, and here was what they saw:

On a pleasant morning in the open air at the remarkable palace of Aksum, teenage twin boys were in fighting sequence training attended by the palace guards. The twin brothers, Prince Ezana and Prince Sayzana wrestled and fought using sticks and then swords. The head of the guards supervised each of their fighting sequences, nodding his head up and down when they did it right.

After the series of fights, the boys sat for their final training, a Gebeta play, which challenged the brain like chess. While they were competing in Gebeta, the massive gate of the palace opened, and soldiers entered guarding two young white boys. The soldiers took the two prisoners to the main chamber of the castle. The twins ceased their Gebeta play and ran after the white boys.

"Let's follow our main characters," the lovebird said as she hopped on Ezana's shoulder.

King Ella Amida was in his chamber consulting with his commerce advisers when his soldiers arrived. The twin princes, the dear children of the king, walked straight to their father and whispered something to him. The king immediately dismissed his advisers to welcome the soldiers who came a long way from the Red Sea. After a brief greeting, King Ella Amida inquired about the two young white boys.

"They are your slaves, Your Majesty," said the leader of the soldiers.

"Where did you get them?" the king asked.

Suddenly, the lovebird made a strange sound, and everybody froze. Before Ezana opened his mouth to ask a question, the lovebird told him to follow her and flew straight to the frozen king. She went behind the king and opened a secret door.

"Come on! Let's go!" the lovebird shouted and jumped into the darkness behind the door.

Ezana had no choice but to follow her. When he walked into the secret door, the dark tunnel flushed him down like the water in a toilet. After a few seconds of speedy travel in the dark tunnel, he saw light and jumped out, roaring. The lovebird waited for him, smiling. Ezana found himself at some shore. His mouth couldn't produce any words, and he stared at the lovebird as if to say, "Where are we at?" She directed him to climb to a tree and wait for something.

A combination of well-armed cavalry, infantry, and navy soldiers of the Kingdom of Aksum galloped from the port city of Adulis and arrived at the shores of the Red Sea. But the group of pirates reported to the army wasn't there. The pirates left a burning ship, dead men, and two young white boys behind. "Bring them to me dead or alive," the angry army commander screamed to his navy soldiers.

The soldiers left immediately on boats to hunt for the pirates. Helpless young, white boys were shaking and crying after the pirates attacked their boat and killed their uncle, who was their guardian and mentor. The soldiers helped the boys to bury their uncle in their Christian faith then took them as prisoners.

The lovebird led Ezana to the same spot where they touched down when they arrived at the shore, and the divine gate that miraculously brought them there took them back to the palace. Ezana wished to spend time on the beautiful coast, but everything happened too quickly.

The lovebird activated the frozen scene, and the episode of the king and the white boys continued:

"Ezana, Sayzana, go play outside," the king ordered his little boys.

The twin princes left without questioning their father's command.

"This pirates attack is the third time this year. How did you let them play around my territory like that?" King Ella Amida roared at the army commander.

"We are hunting them down as far as they go. It won't happen again, Your Majesty," the commander replied while in a bowing position.

"I want this monkey business to end as soon as possible," the king commanded and dismissed the army commander and his soldiers.

"What are your names?" the king asked the young boys.

"I'm Edesius, and he is Frumentius," replied the older boy.

"Welcome to the Kingdom of Aksum. Where are you from, and where was your final destination?" the king asked the boys.

They told him they were from Tyre, and their destination was India. The king asked them more questions about the purpose of their journey and their deceased uncle. They explained to him that their uncle was a Christian, a philosopher, and a merchant. He took them on the trip because he was their guardian and teacher.

"You had an unfortunate week. You are exhausted too. Go take a good rest now," said the king, and he ordered the master of his royal household to send them to a guesthouse.

"They are waiting for you at the coin mint factory, Your Majesty," the master of the royal household reminded the king.

The king walked out of his chamber. His head of guards, along with some soldiers, followed him. The king's sons, Prince Ezana and Prince Saizana, saw their father leave and quit their training to follow him to the factory.

In the hot and noisy factory, the king passed by many smiths working hard on gold and copper mint. His advisor of commerce greeted him with a handful of new minted coins with the king's headshot on them. After examining the fancy new coins of both gold and copper, the king gave his approval.

Prince Ezana begged the advisor of commerce to give him the sample coins. The advisor put the coins in Ezana's pocket when the king started walking out of the factory. Prince Ezana ran back to the palace with the sample coins, and his twin, Prince Sayzana, ran after him to take his share.

The king hopped on the elephant's back to visit an under-construction stela at the skirts of Aksum. His soldiers, advisors, and servants followed him on fifteen elephants on the excursion. On their round trip to and from the quarry place, the king inspected his people transporting obelisks using many giant elephants.

After the visit, the king, joined by his close advisors, wise men, and local and international merchants, sat for lunch at an outdoor terrace facing the stelae park. The king ordered his master of the household to invite the new slaves to join them.

The young white boys came out and bowed to the king. He let them sit, and they were interviewed by the wise men, merchants, and advi-sors. The boys answered all of questions in a way that impressed the king. He thought they were well-educated young boys with noble manners. The next day, the king assigned the boys to work for him in the palace. Quickly, they proved their loyalty and productivity to the king. Then he promoted them as cupbearer and treasurer.

33

STUDYING THE FORBIDDEN

The lovebird kept taking Ezana through essential pieces of history related to the topic "King Ezana and Christianity." She walked him through the history of how King Ezana was baptized into Christianity and converted his entire Aksumite Kingdom to the faith. Every time Ezana complimented the lovebird on how magical and miraculous the experience that was, she granted him another piece of history.

On a delightful Sunday evening at the Aksum palace park, Prince Ezana saw Frumentius reading a book under a big fig tree. He strolled toward him without making any noise. The prince stood behind him for a while, listening to the sound Frumentius made when reading. He couldn't understand the meaning, but he fancied his speed of reading.

After he finished reading, Frumentius kissed the book. Then he saw the prince standing right behind him.

"Oh, Jesus Christ!" Frumentius startled. He stood up and bowed to the crown prince.

"Who's Jesus Christ?" Prince Ezana asked.

Frumentius hid the book in his pocket. "I'll introduce Him to you sometime in the future, your royal highness. What are you doing out here?"

The prince took out a gold coin from his pocket. "Teach me how to read like you."

"God bless you," Frumentius murmured and refused the offer. "I'll teach

you for free, my prince. You may come here every Sunday at this time."
Prince Ezana beamed and jumped happily.

When Frumentius and the prince left the big tree in a thrill, the lovebird turned to Ezana. "Do you want to jump down, or do you want me to forward it to next week?"

"Please forward it," Ezana replied, sitting comfortably on a branch of the big tree.

As promised, Frumentius arrived before the prince.

The lovebird saw the prince coming from afar. "Your namesake is coming," she said.

Ezana nodded and saw Prince Ezana walking like a stalker toward the tree, smiling.

The prince saw his future mentor reading standing up, and the prince waited until he finished. Frumentius finished reading, closed the book and prayed with his eyes closed. When he opened his eyes and kissed the book, the prince moved closer. Frumentius bowed to greet the prince. Prince Ezana waved his hand to disapprove of the bowing. Both sat under the shadow of the tree to start the study.

First, Frumentius gave the prince some pointers on how to develop deep reading techniques. Then he read him a few passages from the Holy Bible, and that way, he introduced him to the Lord Jesus Christ and His mother, St. Mary.

The prince fell in love with the Holy Bible, the Lord, and His mother. He started reading by himself slowly but with great interest and passion. Frumentius listened to each word he pronounced so that he could correct him when he made mistakes.

While the prince and his mentor were lost reading under the beautiful tree, from the top of the tree, the lovebird and Ezana saw soldiers marching from the palace. The soldiers got closer, but Frumentius and

Prince Ezana didn't see or hear them. Ezana was worried and asked the lovebird to do something, but she said she couldn't edit history.

When the soldiers entered the shadow of the big fig tree, Frumentius heard their footsteps, turned around, and saw the two soldiers armed with their swords racing toward them. Frumentius snatched the Holy Bible from Ezana's hands, hid it in his pocket, and jumped to his feet.

"I apologize, my prince," Frumentius whispered to Ezana as polite as possible.

"I love everything you taught me today. Thank you," Ezana whispered back.

The soldiers approached.

"White boy, His Majesty, the king, wants to see you in the palace at once," said one of the soldiers.

When Frumentius started walking, Prince Ezana followed him. The soldiers escorted them from behind.

"What do you think it's all about?" asked the young prince.

"Practicing Christianity is forbidden in the kingdom. Reading the Holy Bible in the palace is a crime. It could cost me my life, your royal highness," Frumentius whispered.

"But I didn't tell my father about it. I won't tell him." Ezana said.

"God bless you, my prince."

Ezana jumped off the tree. "I want to see what that's about."

The lovebird landed on his shoulder, and they followed behind the soldiers to the palace.

Greek merchants were good friends to the king brought expensive presents of silk, carpets, and oil lamps for the king and his family. To honor his guests, the king ordered dinner and wine served early. The king was laughing with his guests when soldiers escorted Frumentius into the dining room.

"White boy, bring good wines for my good friends!" the king shouted.

Frumentius exhaled in relief and went off to the wine cellar. At the end of the dinner, the king ordered his treasurer, Edesius, to present copper, gold, and ivory gifts for his guests.

34

TURNING PRINCES TO PRIESTS

On the next Sunday, Prince Ezana brought his twin brother, Prince Saizana, with him to join the secret reading session. A super happy Frumentius taught them the basics of reading. Then he narrated some passages from both the Old and the New Testaments of the Holy Bible.

"Genesis 1," Frumentius started reading and narrated to the princes how God created the universe in six days. He concluded, "God was pleased by all that He created, and on the seventh day, God rested."

The princes followed him with their undivided attention.

"The power of God is fascinating," said Prince Ezana.

Both princes encouraged Frumentius to tell them more stories.

"Genesis 2," continued Frumentius. "This will be the last chapter for today." He narrated the story of Adam and Eve.

Finally, Saizana begged Frumentius to tell him what he described to Ezana the other day about Jesus Christ. Frumentius couldn't say no to the prince, and he loved to tell the story of Jesus Christ. He looked at Prince Ezana for approval, and Ezana encouraged him to tell the story again.

"Book of Luke," began Frumentius. "There was a virgin named Mary who lived in the town of Nazareth in Galilee. She loved God dearly. She was to marry a man named Joseph.

"God sent the angel, Gabriel, to tell her that she had found favor with God and that He would cause her to become pregnant while she was still a virgin. *She accepted this, and so she became pregnant. Gabriel also visited Joseph and told him what God desired so that he would not think Mary had been unfaithful."*

And Frumentius continued reading passages about how Jesus Christ was born in Bethlehem. When done for the day, he folded the Holy Bible and kissed it. Before he deposited it into his pocket, Prince Ezana asked to do the same, and Frumentius let him kiss the Holy Bible. Saizana followed his brother and kissed the Holy Bible also.

"It's time for the entertainment program," Frumentius said, dismissing the class under the tree.

The princes thanked him and started to run to the amphitheater. Frumentius followed them after a brief prayer alone.

35

MORE MIND-BLOWING EXPERIENCES

W hat's next?" Ezana asked the lovebird, swinging his legs on the branch of the tree.

"We can forward another week and watch them study, or we can join them at the amphitheater. Your choice," the lovebird said, spreading both wings.

"What's at the amphitheater?"

"The king with his family and friends like to enjoy special entertainment," the lovebird said. "Once every month, the king brings entertainers from Greek, Roma, China, and Egypt. That's why they call it special."

Ezana jumped down from the tree with a sudden flame of desire to see the entertainment.

"And the monthly show happens today?" he asked.

"It's about to start in a few minutes." The lovebird landed on his shoulder, and Ezana marched to the venue. He was so eager that he avoided the cobbled pathway and took a short cut over the green field.

"Relax. We can go back and forth in time. We can rewind, forward, pause, and play the events," the lovebird reminded him.

Ezana stopped walking and took a moment to recognize the power God gave to the lovebird. He witnessed when she did pretty much all of them.

"You are absolutely right." He went back on the track of the cobbled pathway and started walking, relaxed.

"And do you want to experience something you never expected?" the lovebird asked.

"Everything happening so far I have never imagined. I don't think you have something more surprising left."

She looked at him as if to say, "Oh, yeah?" And she chirped and waited. Ezana stopped and looked around him to see something. But what happened blew Ezana's mind. A sensational voice resembling Morgan Freeman started narrating about the secret Bible study that took place every Sunday evening under the fig tree.

The voice of the narrator said this:

Frumentius carried the Bible studies of the princes every Sunday under the tree for a long time. Sometimes, the treasurer of the king and Frumentius's brother, Edesius, who was a good preacher himself, joined them under the tree. Two white slave brothers teaching the two prince brothers a foreign religion was unusual, noticeable, and dangerous. Therefore, they changed the venue to a basement room administrated by Edesius.

However, Queen Sophia, the princes' mother, found out about the secret studies. She investigated the matter without informing the king. One Sunday evening, the queen surprised them while the white boys were teaching her sons a foreign religion.

Frumentius and Edesius trembled when they saw the queen step down into the underground room, which they never imagined she would. All of them jumped to their feet and capitulated politely in front of the queen.

Without much ado, the queen sat among them and asked the white boys to explain what they were teaching her sons. Pleasantly surprised, the white boys described their teachings of Christianity with grace and compassion.

The queen listened to both of them calmly and said, "My sons became well-behaved since they started this study."

All beamed from the queen's remarks.

"I want you to keep your study but keep it quiet." She smiled at them and left.

That day marked a new hope for Christianity on the horizon.

36

KING ELLA AMIDA'S SPECIAL
ENTERTAINMENT

Around a thousand people sat in the amphitheater staring at the half-circled stage, eagerly waiting to be entertained. Ezana sat ten rows behind the exclusive seats reserved for the king and his families. He surveyed how the semi-circular amphitheater was built. *A Greek architecture concept and Aksumite structure,* he thought.

"Every month, top local and foreign artists and magicians showcase their best acts here. If the king likes it, he lets the people enjoy the entertainment free of charge on the biggest amphitheater outside of the palace," the lovebird said.

"You mean there is another amphitheater in the city?" Ezana asked.

"Holds thousands of people," the lovebird said with pride.

"Cool."

Suddenly, the audience stopped talking. A man appeared on the stage and announced the king's arrival. Everybody shot up. A lion and a lioness walked in followed by the royal army guards. Then King Ella Amida, Queen Sophia, Prince Ezana, Prince Sayzana, and the king's close advisors entered. The people cheered for the royal family. The king gave them a sign to sit, and then the extraordinary show of the month commenced.

The spectators applauded for equestrian shows, staged battles, trained animals, jugglers, and acrobats of local and foreign artists. Mostly, the audience followed the king. When the king clapped, smiled, or laughed, the audience mimicked him. Then the most anticipated part of the show started— the comedy.

The audience became excited and sat on the edge of their seats. Some comedians performed their original jokes. Some of them told old jokes of Lysistrata, the Greek comedian, and Terence from Roman. People laughed so hard. The king, known for his love of humor, wiped tears of laughter from his face several times. On one particular joke about the Pharaoh, the king stood up from his golden throne and laughed so hard that the lions startled. Then he walked out, laughing.

The lions, guards, his family, and advisors followed him. The show wasn't over yet, but the king didn't anticipate any joke would top the one about the Pharaoh. And when the king left, the show was supposed to be over. So, the audience dispersed. The artists who didn't get the chance to perform were devastated.

Ezana enjoyed the event, and he found it delicious to contemplate on the way back to the palace. He always loved comedy, but he didn't know that the craft had a history of delighting the hearts of humankind that long.

However, people were laughing hysterically, so Ezana missed most of the contents of the jokes. He became curious about the last comedy bit that made the king walkout laughing harder. He asked the lovebird.

"You mean you didn't get that joke?"

"Everybody was too loud, you know," Ezana said.

The lovebird seemed happy to tell the joke, and her face beamed.

"How do you entertain a bored Pharaoh? You sail a boatload of young women dressed only in fishing nets down the Nile and urge the Pharaoh to go catch a fish. It's an old joke, but it always works." She giggled.

"Seriously? That makes you laugh too?" Ezana said, looking at the lovebird quizzically.

"It's hilarious. Do you think you can do better?"

Ezana thought about the old jokes some of the comedians did. It was the mid-4th century. He imagined how they would react to the jokes from his era.

"I would, but I don't want people to die laughing." Ezana chuckled.

The lovebird hovered in front of him and stared at his eyes as if to say, "Seriously?"

"What? They are laughing out loud at four-hundred-year-old jokes. They will go crazy if I tell them some of the funny jokes of our time," Ezana said, and he went around her bragging.

She turned and flew after him. "I can put you on stage, you know."

"With the funny materials of the hilarious comedians of my era, it will be a walk in the park." He walked like it. And then he remembered something. "But you said it's a monthly show?"

"And there is a smaller show every Friday exclusive to the royal family. Get ready, and we'll see how you pull that off," the lovebird said excitedly.

"Deal," Ezana said, and his mind already started running through killer bits from his favorite comedians.

A teenager from the twenty-first-century presents his comedy on a 4th-century stage, the lovebird thought.

"Oh! It's going to be exciting," she said.

Ezana stopped again and turned to her with his quizzical look.

"Are you going to change your mind?" the lovebird asked, hovering at his eye level.

"No, but I'm invisible to them. How am I going to perform?"

She landed on his shoulder. "Don't worry about that," she whispered.

Ezana stuffed his hands into his pocket to do his "a walk in the park" act again. His right hand felt something in his pocket. He remembered the chocolate he brought in his pocket, and his face flushed with excitement. He fetched the Snickers bar from his deep pocket, uncovered it, broke it into two, and shared it with the bird.

"Mmmmm," the lovebird said as soon as she put a piece of the chocolate in her mouth. "Who told you I love chocolates?"

Ezana jokingly answered, "A little bird," and they both laughed.

The amphitheater was built inside the palace on the opposite side of the main chambers, which Ezana thought a brilliant idea to avoid noise. They walked halfway and sat on a stone bench by a remarkably cultivated green field. Ezana couldn't help the temptation. He walked into the beautiful greenfield and slid like soccer stars do after scoring goals. The lovebird enjoyed the act.

Ezana laid down on his back on the natural green carpet and stared at the clear blue sky above him. "I think the sky is the only similarity we have with the ancients," Ezana said almost to himself.

"Are you interested in staying for another episode, or do you want to go back to the 21st century?"

"I like to stay in this century." He rolled in the field. "What's next?"

The lovebird suggested forwarding ten years for a vital period in the history of the Aksumite Kingdom. Ezana agreed. They kept walking into the palace and entered into a scene from ten years later.

37

THE KING'S EXTREME DEMAND

King Alla Amida, seriously sick on his bed, ordered his master of the household to bring him his wise men, sorcerers, and a doctor immediately. His wife helped him to sit, and she stood by his side. All the wise men, sorcerers, and the doctor entered following one another. Some of them looked anxious, and some of them looked frightened. They all bowed to both the king and the queen.

The king coughed terribly, which made everyone feel uncomfortable.

"How much time do I have left?" the king asked, struggling with his coughing.

None of them answered, and the king kept coughing.

The queen gazed at all of them. "Silence is not an answer. Wise men?"

The wise men looked at each other.

"We don't know it yet, Your Majesties," their leader said.

"Doctor?" the king shouted.

The doctor shook his head.

"Don't be afraid to tell me what you know." The king turned to the sorcerers.

"We are still working on it, Your Majesty," replied the leader of the sorcerers.

The king, unhappy with their answers, turned his face away from all of them to a wall. The queen gave them the signal to leave the room. They all beamed with relief and left the room quickly.

Queen Sophia paced back and forth in the room. "My king, may I call the white boys for you? They are wise."

The king, still facing the wall, said, "You think they are better than all the wise men, sorcerers, and doctor?" He burst into a sudden laugh, which got him coughing heavily.

The queen walked out of the room and came back with the white boys. The king turned around and stared at them. The boys, now much older, tanned, and stronger bowed and stood with their heads down.

Ezana turned to the lovebird and looked at her, puzzled about the new looks of the white boys.

"That happens when you are exposed to the African sun for ten years," she whispered to him.

"The queen thinks you are wise enough to tell me how long I will live from now," the king said.

"We can't. But our God can, Your Majesty," Edesius said.

"Well, how are we supposed to communicate with your God?" the king asked.

"Your majesty, if you let us pray at the Ark of the Covenant, we may bring you the news," Frumentius said.

The king waved a hand, signaling them to go pray.

The white brothers bowed and left the room.

"My dear Sophia, I know you are worried, but the boys are too immature to know my destiny." The king laughed again, which was instantly replaced by coughing.

The master of the household entered the room and announced, "The army general, Your Majesty."

The general walked in and bowed to the king and the queen. The king struggled to stop coughing. The general waited, standing head down. When the king finally stopped, the army general proudly said, "The Red Sea coast is now free of pirates, Your Majesty."

The king smiled, and the queen and the master of the household grinned. The general cleared his throat and added, "We destroyed them all, Your Majesty." Suddenly, the king felt healthy and alive. He effortlessly sat on his bed by himself.

"Thank You, Lord," the queen muttered.

The army general, encouraged by the positive reactions from the king and the queen, continued, "No one escaped or surrendered alive. The trade route is now safe."

"Well done, general. Now, I'm ready to die," the king said.

38

QUEEN SABA AND THE ARK OF THE COVENANT

The lovebird led Ezana to the miraculous door again, which swept him away into darkness and then into the light. He found himself on top of a bell tower of a temple. He enjoyed a terrific bird's eye view from the top. A temple surrounded by green trees was revealed beneath them.

"No idea why we are here, but I love the view," Ezana said to the lovebird.

"I'm glad you liked it. Just a few seconds."

"For?"

She stretched her wing to show him. The white brothers appeared, walked toward the gate of the temple, and knelt down for prayer.

Ezana didn't know they were on top of the old temple that housed the Ark of the Covenant. Too much was happening, and he forgot about the painting titled "Chapel of the Tablet" in Afewerk Tekle's bedroom. Suddenly, he felt the electric shock he experienced when he touched the painting. Then he heard his mom saying, "You are experiencing a deja vu, baby."

The lovebird interrupted his wandering mind. "I assume you are aware of the Ark of the Covenant," she said.

Ezana hesitated and then nodded.

"And do you know how it ended up here in Aksum?"

"Not much. I Googled about Queen Saba and the Ark, but there was too much stuff on the Internet. Africa, the West, and the Middle East have interests in both the queen and the Ark," he said, showing interest in listening to her version.

"I sense you want to hear the story, and I'm thrilled because the story involves my species." She chirped and put the narrator on.

Queen Saba was a powerful, wise, wealthy, and beautiful queen of Aksum. Her power, wealth, and intelligence were widely known all over the world. The most prominent king of the time, Solomon, the wise
king of Israel who was chosen to build the House of Lord, heard legends of the African queen too. He used Hoopoe, his well-trained bird, to communicate with the queen.

After exchanging a few letters, the wealthy and wise king invited the queen to visit his kingdom and the House of the Lord he built in Jerusalem. Driven by a thirst for knowledge and wisdom, the curious queen traveled from her capital Aksum to Jerusalem. Alongside two hundred caravans and hundreds of servants and soldiers, the queen journeyed thousands of kilometers through the desert.

When Queen Saba reached the famous King Solomon's palace in Jerusalem, she gave him lots of gifts he had never seen before of spices, gold, and precious stones. Then they quickly engaged in philosophical conversations. She asked him tons of questions, and he answered all of them. His wisdom took her breath away.

King Solomon gave Queen Saba an exclusive tour around the House of the Lord he built for God. The grace of the Temple of God blew her mind.

The wise king himself was impressed by the wisdom and curiosity of the African queen too. Soon, they became a fan of each other and intimate. Their long conversations over food and wine sparked romance. As a result, Menelik I, the son of King Solomon and Queen Saba, was born.

Menelik was raised by his mother in Aksum. Many years later, when Menelik came of age, he traveled to Jerusalem to visit his father. The wise King Solomon was thrilled to see his son for the first time. Though Solomon expected him to remain in Israel to be the next king, Menelik preferred to become the first Solomonic dynasty king of Aksum.

Upon his return from Jerusalem to Aksum, Menelik brought the Ark of the Covenant with him. His father also gave him many Israelites to assist him in ruling according to biblical standards.

The lovebird stopped the narration and looked at Ezana. "So?" she asked him.

"I never heard about the bird, Hoopoe. Plus, the public knowledge out there is Queen Saba initiated the visit to Jerusalem. Never heard or read King Solomon communicated with her via his trained bird," Ezana said.

"For truth, you have to dig deeper."

"You are right. Maybe it's because birds don't care to take credit for their contributions," Ezana said jokingly.

"Hoopoe was one of the chosen ones," the lovebird said respectfully.

"Hoopoe must have traveled thousands of miles back and forth."

"Yes, but compared to Paul the apostle, it's a walk in the sky park, as you might say," the lovebird said.

"How far did Paul travel?" Ezana asked.

"More than 10,000 miles on foot."

"Wow! Why did he travel that much?"

"To preach that Jesus is the Son of God," the lovebird said.

After praying on their knees in unison, Frumentius and Edesius, got up and started going back to the palace. The lovebird signaled for Ezana to follow her. In a few seconds, they reappeared inside the large room of King Ella Amida.

39

THE EMANCIPATION OF THE WHITE SLAVES

The king was in a pleasant mood when the brothers entered.
He received them well. "So, did you communicate with your God," the king asked. "I hope he didn't ignore my case."

The white brothers stayed head down until the king finished talking.

"Our great God is so kind. He responded to our prayers instantly," Frumentius said in a polite tone.

The king became attentive. "Well, I'm in a good mood to take any bad news now, so you better hurry," said the king, sipping his Chinese tea.

Frumentius turned to Edesius to break the news to the king, but Edesius hesitated.

The king stopped sipping the tea and concentrated on the brothers. "Go ahead. Don't be afraid to tell me what you have. I'm not going to believe it anyway."

Queen Sophia nodded her head up and down, encouraging Edesius to speak up.

"I'm afraid you do not have much time, Your Majesty," Edesius said.

The king burst into laughter. The queen gave a signal to the white brothers to leave the room.

"How much time do I have?" the king shouted.

Halfway on their way out of the extra-large room, the brothers stopped and turned toward the king.

"Not much, Your Majesty," Frumentius murmured in a trembling voice.

"I said, 'How long?' I need a precise answer!" the king yelled.

"According to our God, two days at most, Your Majesty."

The king burst into laughter again. The white brothers walked the rest of the way out of the room.

Suddenly, the king felt some pain in his stomach and stopped laughing involuntarily. He started groaning in pain. The queen ordered the master of the household to bring the doctor promptly.

Ezana looked at the lovebird for what was going on, but she acted as she didn't understand.

"Do you want to leave?"

"Are you kidding me? This is the climax," Ezana said.

The lovebird giggled, and she forwarded the scene a little bit.

The queen sat on the bed next to the king, massaging his paled face with a soaked cloth. The doctor couldn't stop the king's pain and aimlessly walked back and forth in the room. The wise men awkwardly stood around the king's bed. The king kept vomiting, tossing, and groaning.

During unpleasant time, the white brothers walked in and bowed to the king and queen and all of the noblemen.

"The white boys are here, Your Majesty," the master of the household announced.

The brothers didn't have any idea why they were called back, but they prepared themselves for the worst: death or prison.

The king gave them a hand signal to get closer to him. They paced toward him and bowed down again.

In a weak voice, the king said, "You are honorable and obedient boys. You served me with integrity and compassion. My family and I are very grateful to you..." he interrupted his speech and coughed.

"From now on..." the king continued, "...from now on, you are free men. Free to go back to your country. The master of the royal household will handle your farewell."

In a delightful surprise, the brothers looked at each other with smiles of happiness.

"Serving you and your beloved family was an honor, Your Majesty," Edesuis said.

"My brother is right. You and your family treated us with kindness and compassion. Thank you, Your Majesties," Frumentius added.

The brothers bowed down again to the king and the queen and left the room.

The king stared at the ceiling in complete silence. He exhaled and said, "Bring my sons Ezana and Sayzana to me."

The lovebird whispered to Ezana to follow the white brothers. Ezana walked out of the large room of the king, turned right after the white brothers, and walked down a long hallway to the two-story buildings on the right-wing of the castle. At the end of the hall, they took stairs down behind the brothers into one of the basement houses. The brothers got into their shared room.

Ezana surveyed the paintings of Jesus Christ, St. Mary, and many angels in the brothers' room. Similar to my dad's childhood room, he thought.

"Praise the Lord, we are going home, brother," Edesius said, grinning broadly.

Frumentius opened his arms wide and hugged him. Then both knelt, prayed, and thanked God for their freedom.

"But brother, I feel we have unfinished business," Frumentius said.

"What business are you talking about?" Edesius asked.

"The Bible studies with the princes. Now, they are the future, and we can Christen the whole kingdom," Frumentius said passionately.

"I agree, but our service is not needed anymore. With the help of God, the good boys will take it from here," Edesius said with less appetite to continue the conversation.

Suddenly, a noise of people crying echoed in the basement corridors.

"The king is dead," Edesius said.

40

A MYSTERY RIDE EZANA COULDN'T SOLVE

The next day, Ezana found himself in bed at his grandparents' house. Lying on his bed, he tried to think about what happened the night before. He remembered how he met the lovebird and every moment of the magical experience in the extraordinary night, but he couldn't remember how he got back home and into his bed. He went back again and again to the last moment he recalled, trying to connect the missing link, but his brain couldn't connect the dots. It bothered him so much that he jumped out of his bed to go out to meet the bird.

However, his parents were back from their brief trip, and they were in the living room waiting for him. He was happy to see them, but his happiness evaporated when he realized that it would be difficult for him to meet the lovebird anytime he wanted. He gave his dad and mom hugs.

His mom noticed a melancholy mood on his face. "You don't seem happy to see us. What's wrong?"

"That tells me you enjoyed my parents more than your own parents," Yared chuckled.

Ezana's grandma cleared her throat, which was her polite signal to ask permission to talk. Everyone understood that and waited for her to speak.

"He is a lovely boy. His presence brought tremendous joy to our home," she said.

Ezana's grandpa nodded his head up and down, expressing his satisfaction with the remark his wife made. Ezana saw an opportunity in his grandparents' comments, and he wanted to seize the opportunity.

"I liked it here. Grandma and Grandpa are awesome. I want to be with them for the rest of our stay in Aksum," he said firmly.

His grandparents grinned with their half toothless mouths.

"Wow! I'm thrilled to hear that, son," Yared said.

"I'm thrilled too, but how about the Internet? I was worried you would want Internet access badly," Tsehay said.

Ezana shrugged his shoulders. "I didn't miss it yet. I like the praying rituals with Grandpa and Grandma."

His happy grandparents showered him with more blessings. His parents couldn't believe how fast their boy changed from a game addict brat to a wise boy.

"Well," Yared said, and turned to his wife.

"Okay. Great," Tsehay said, still amazed.

"Thanks. I'll go with you to the hotel for a shower and come back in the evening," Ezana said.

Ezana and his parents walked to the Yeha Hotel. Ezana hastened into his parents' room. He took a shower and left to look for the lovebird. The lovebird wasn't there. He sat at the usual spot, the most beautiful view in Aksum, hoping she would come soon.

In the meantime, he continued to solve the puzzle of how he got home after his miraculous journey to the 4th century. He tried hard, but he still couldn't reach the point that could take him there. The last thing he could remember from the magical experience was when King Ella Amida freed the white brothers from slavery.

"Ezana, I'll see you tonight. Same time, same place," the lovebird cried in the sky above him.

"Hey, come down! I want to ask you something," Ezana shouted.

"I have to be somewhere. I'm already late. And don't forget to bring me chocolate." She flew away. Her last phrase made him smile, and he went to the hotel room to grab some chocolates.

Ezana snuck out of his grandparents' house and arrived at the meeting place before midnight. The lovebird saw him coming from one of the Aksumite stelae. She flew down without making any sound and landed on his shoulder quietly.

"Jesus Christ! You scared the crap out of me!" Ezana shouted.

The lovebird exploded in a peal of laughter on his reaction. Though he panicked, he couldn't miss observing the beauty of her laughter. She used both her wings, her eyes, her legs, and her voice. She brought her everything to produce mesmerizing laughter like a great composer who used an orchestra to create a piece of great music.

"Did you bring the chocolate?" she asked.

Ezana searched all of his pockets. "Oh, I forgot to put some in my pocket."

The lovebird transformed into a hummingbird and flew back and forth on his eye level. "You must be kidding me!" she cried.

Ezana laughed out loud. "Look at your face? You are so pissed off!"

She realized he was making fun of her. "Oh, I love chocolates, especially the dark ones," she said passionately.

"In that case, this is your lucky day. I got you some dark chocolates." He broke a bar into pieces and fed them her.

"Now, let's go watch history," said the lovebird, beaming with pleasure.

Ezana started walking, following the light she provided. "This is unbelievable, you know."

"Which part is unbelievable?" she asked.

"Everything. You, the time machine, and the magic door to the ancient kingdom," Ezana said, running through all of the unbelievable experiences in his head.

"God created the universe and every life in it. He created you and me. He created the people who invented great things that you admire. Why is it unbelievable to believe that God could make a bird talk or a time machine taking you through the history of the world?" the lovebird asked.

Ezana scratched his head. "You are right. I meant nobody will believe me if I tell them the miracles I am experiencing right now."

The lovebird took another bite of chocolate and did extra chewing to prolong the joy of the deliciousness in her mouth.

"What's in John 20:29?" the lovebird asked.

Ezana didn't know the answer. *You would know it if you have read the Bible more than the comic books*, he said to himself.

The lovebird swallowed the chocolate and spoke in an even sweeter tone than before. *"Because you have seen me, you have believed; blessed are those who have not seen and yet have believed."*

Ezana nodded. He heard his mom refer to that verse many times.

"And don't bother whether people will believe you are not. Just enjoy the blessings from God."

"I hear you," Ezana said.

"Good boy."

"One more thing."

"I'm listening."

"I couldn't remember how I got home yesterday or into my bed, for that matter. Any idea?" Ezana asked.

"I'm glad you asked. I'll tell you later if you stay awake," the lovebird said.

"Okay, cool."

They arrived at the entrance early. Ezana sat on the stairs made up of large stones until the clock turned to 1:00 A.M. The sophisticated gate opened in the same stylish fashion as the previous night. The lovebird touched some features, and the two-seater sled popped out.

After a speedy journey through darkness and light, they entered into the kingdom of the past.

"Right on time," the lovebird said as soon as they touched down.

"Wow! What's that wave?" Ezana asked.

"Let's go see."

41

THE KING'S FUNERAL

Members of the royal family, all the noblemen and noblewomen of the kingdom, wise men, smith men, craftsmen, artisans, philosophers, local and international merchants, soldiers, habitants of the city of Aksum, magicians, the white brothers, and many exotic animals, including elephants and lions, escorted King Ella Amida's body from the palace to the stelae park. A chariot carried the deceased king, and all followed on foot.

The body rested in a tent shed at the park. One of the wise men came forward and gave a hand signal to the crowd. Everybody stopped crying instantly. Then he delivered a long but appealing eulogy. Representatives of all societies also made speeches in a hierarchy order about the king's outstanding personality and noble achievements.

Then the master of the funeral ceremony announced all to bid their final farewell to their beloved king. Soldiers unloaded the body of their king from the chariot and put him in the royal family's mausoleum. The extraordinary funeral ceremony of King Ella Amida, King of the Aksumite Kingdom, came to an end.

The crowd started to disperse in beautiful forms, which looked like something designed by an artistic director.

***

"Wow! They knew how to pull off a remarkable ceremony," Ezana whispered.

"I know," the lovebird replied. "Let's follow the white brothers."

The white brothers walked to the palace behind the chariots of the royal family.

"What now?" Frumentius asked his brother.

"It's time to pack and leave, brother," replied Edesius with a smile.

To their amazement, a messenger horseman approached them.

"Her Majesty, the queen, wants to see you both in her chamber," the horseman said. He rode back toward the royal family without giving them a chance to reply.

42

CORONATION OF KING EZANA

The exhausted and paled Queen Sophia welcomed the white brothers in her chamber. She always treated them well, even when they were slaves. Now, as free young men, she showed them more respect and asked them to join her for tea. She showed them the way to the beautiful garden behind her chamber.

The queen herself planted, cultivated, and beautified the garden. Only those she adored and loved the most were welcomed in the garden. Her husband, the late king, used to call it the "Garden of the Queen."

"I'll join you in a minute," the queen said and went back to give orders to the master of the royal household.

Edesius didn't like the queen's extra kindness toward them because he suspected that she might be up to something. Frumentius's prayer was the opposite. While the white brothers waited for the queen, the chef of the queen served the brothers local bread, hibishti, and tea, which became their favorite since they arrived in the kingdom.

"I didn't know hibishti had history this long," Ezana whispered to the lovebird.

"It was invented here way, way before chocolate, and it's much healthier too," the lovebird replied, jumping from flower to flower in the beautiful garden.

Frumentius and Edasius prayed before they start eating.

"Ah, I'm going to miss this," Edasius said, chewing a mouthful of the hibishti.

"I'm glad to hear that because you are not going to," the queen said from behind.

"Your Majesty," they both muttered at the same time, shot up, and bowed down.

"Please sit and enjoy your snacks," she said. "I asked you to come on this inconvenient time because I was afraid you might leave without saying goodbye."

"We wouldn't do that, Your Majesty," Frumentius replied graciously.

"Is there anything we can do before we leave, Your Majesty?" asked Edasius in a trembling voice.

"You are free young men now. You don't have any responsibilities to the kingdom as slaves. But I ask you as mentors of my sons and good friends of the kingdom to extend your stay until my son, Prince Ezana, grows up to become a king." The queen picked up her cup of tea and sipped it while hoping to hear a good response.

The brothers didn't respond promptly.

The queen put the teacup back on the timber table and added some lines she believed would help. "My sons like you so much, and they don't want you to leave. If you stay, I'll promote you to honorable positions," the queen concluded and waited for their answers.

The brothers took a moment to communicate with each other with their eyes.

"It would be a pleasure and an honor to serve the kingdom for more years, Your Majesty. But we kindly ask you to allow us to exercise and preach our faith freely in public," Frumentius said politely.

The queen beamed with delight.

"That's a deal, and let's shake hands for that."

They shook hands, and the queen left them to enjoy the rest of their hibishti and tea. The white brothers exchanged hugs to celebrate their freedom to exercise and preach their faith in one of the mighty empires in the world. Now, they were more ecstatic to stay in the kingdom and practice their faith in Christianity than to go back home.

Ezana and the lovebird exited the garden and walked around the palace aimlessly. Everybody was grieving the death of the king, and the vibe was cold.

"The people must have loved the king," Ezana said.

"They did. Ella Amida was a fun-loving king," the lovebird said.

"He looked charming," Ezana said, walking through a gate.

"You are leaving the palace," the lovebird alerted him.

Ezana shrugged and continued exiting from the palace. It was too cold for him. He wanted the fun side of the kingdom.

"Speaking of fun, when are you going to let me perform my comedy act?" Ezana asked.

"Anytime you are ready with your material."

"Awesome. I'll work on it."

They kept walking, and Ezana asked the lovebird to put audio narration on as they walked.

"Wonderful idea," the lovebird said, and the incredible voice of the narrator appeared all around Ezana.

The white brothers continued serving the queen, the princes, and the kingdom in several capacities. They changed the Bible study classroom from under the fig tree and the basement to one of the beautiful gardens in the palace. They taught Christianity to Prince Ezana and Prince Saizana in an open environment. The queen also joined the Bible study as often as possible.

Christian merchants who would come to the kingdom for trading used to practice their Christian religion clandestinely. Praise to God and thanks to the brothers, the kingdom allowed them to practice their faith in public.

A few years after King Ella Amida died, Ezana came of age. Queen Sophia ordered the kingdom to prepare an incredible ceremony for her son's day of coronation. Thousands of distinguished guests and friends of the kingdom were invited from near and far. Magicians and artisans performed their best acts. The monarch provided memorabilia for all the guests. Local and international chefs exhibited their exquisite domestic and foreign food and drinks.

On a delightful day in the city of Aksum and in an extraordinary ceremony, Prince Ezana was coronated king of the Aksumite Kingdom.

"May this please the people of our kingdom," King Ezana declared. "God bless you all." The phrase "God bless you all" was heard for the first time and remained in the kingdom after that.

The festivity of the coronation continued for days with a variety of entertainment, food, and drinks.

Listening to the narration, the lovebird on his shoulder, Ezana continued walking the cobbled street beneath tall palm trees. Part of the description of the food reminded him of the hibishti he saw in the queen's garden, and he craved it.

"Is there any way we can get hibishti?" he asked the lovebird.

"There is a popular place where people go every day. It's so fresh and delicious. Usually, it gets sold out before everyone buys," the lovebird said passionately.

"If that's the case, how are we going to get one?" Ezana asked.

"Ahem, ahem." The lovebird cleared her throat. "Look at the birds of the air. They do not sow or reap or store away in barns, and yet your heavenly Father feeds them. Are you not much more valuable than they?" She sighed in satisfaction. "We the birds are mentioned twenty times in the Bible, but I love that verse. It's my favorite."

Ezana thought he asked a smart question, but he felt stupid when he heard the answer.

"Great answer," he said sheepishly.

Ezana followed the lovebird's directions to the hibishti shop. The streets of Aksum were quiet due to the mourning of the king. Shops closed, the open markets were gone, and only a few people were active.

"Ezana, stop!" the lovebird shouted.

"What? What?" Ezana startled and stopped.

"Look down," the lovebird cried.

Ezana looked down at the cobbled road, and he saw a coin. She told him to pick it up.

"You scared me," he said, picking up the silver coin.

"I'm sorry. I was excited. Keep going."

Ezana continued strolling. Arriving at the end of the road, he heard people coming back complaining about the closed hibishti shop. After the Bible verse mentioned by the lovebird, Ezana believed she would get some miraculously, and he kept walking to the closed shop. The air brought him a smell the aroma of the freshly baked hibishti.

"Oh! It smells delicious!" he exclaimed.

To Ezana's surprise, he saw a woman opening the hibishti house when they got closer. The lovebird whispered in his ear and jumped off his shoulder to a nearby tree. Ezana laughed like a fool when she told him to buy hibishti with the coin he picked up on the way.

Ezana dipped his hand into a nearby water garden. He became visible and walked to the hibishti shop corner.

"A marathon of miracles," he murmured and put the coin in the woman's hand.

She handed him a freshly baked hibishti while gazing at him suspiciously.

The lovebird jumped back on Ezana's shoulder, and they disappeared before the woman formed a word.

"Have I just sold to an alien?" the woman mumbled. People who craved hibishti woke her up from the daydream-like experience.

43

A SUPER BIRTHDAY SURPRISE!

Ezana and the lovebird stopped at the stelae park to enjoy both the view and their fresh Hibishti. They sat on a stone bench facing the exquisitely carved standing obelisks raised above flowers and trees.

"Wow! The stelae park looks more impressive in its old age than in the present day," Ezana said.

"It's old age for you but not for the obelisks. They are younger and stronger here," the lovebird said.

Ezana got the point and nodded instead of speaking with his mouth full. Suddenly, he saw delighted people moving in and around the park and gazed at the lovebird, puzzled.

"Oh, good. You noticed," she swallowed. "I forwarded us a little bit into King Ezana's golden period so that we can see the glorious period of the monuments. That's why you are looking at happy people.

And wait... one, two three! Boom! Surprise! Happy birthday!"

Suddenly, the exquisite King Ezana's stele appeared right in front of Ezana. He lit up and stood up, his eyes and mouth wide open in awe.

"Thanks a lot! You are the best. How about a little walk in this wonderful park?" Ezana asked, grinning.

"Sure. Meet you up there, birthday boy," the lovebird flew up to the top of King Ezana's stele and looked down.

Ezana stood up under the elegant stele erected by his namesake. He walked around it in admiration. The lovebird joined him, and they walked gently inside the park, smelling the fragrances of the plants and flowers, looking up all of the towering obelisks.

No one in the park could disregard the sleeping giant, possibly the most massive monolithic stele that ancient humans ever attempted to erect. When Ezana and the lovebird gazed at the thirty-three-meter long stele that laid across the park, an idea struck Ezana, and he smiled.

"I know what you are thinking, and my answer is no," the lovebird said.

"Why not? Please?" Ezana begged.

"That was the most tragic moment in the history of the Aksumite Kingdom. You can't handle it."

Ezana read extreme sadness on her eyes. He stared at the fallen obelisk and imagined the degree of the tragic accident during the effort to erect the massive monolithic stele.

"I'm sorry, Ezana. Maybe next time when you turn eighteen," the lovebird said in a melancholy voice.

"I understand."

They stayed a little while in the golden era walking around the stelae park and the royal tombs.

Suddenly, Ezana's face lit up.

"What?" the lovebird asked.

"My dad loves talking about his namesake more than anything. He says Yared is the most under-appreciated musical genius on the planet. Yared not only wrote and composed music more than a thousand years before Mozart and Beethoven were born, but Dad thinks Yared also introduced the art of conducting to the world. He passionately tells the story of Yared over and over. I used to wish that Dad was Ezana and I was named after Yared," Ezana said.

"And now?"

"It's an honor to be called Ezana after the incredible king," Ezana said, still lit up.

"Happy to hear that. Time to go back to the 21st century."

44

FROM TINY TO GIGANTIC

Ezana and the lovebird got back in the 21st century at lightning speed, and they found themselves climbing up the stone stairs from the palace of King Kaleb.

"I'm dying to know how I got home yesterday. Please tell me," asked Ezana when they got out of the underground of the palace.

"Are you sure you want to know?"

"One-hundred percent."

The lovebird jumped from his shoulder down to the floor. "Close your eyes and turn around."

Ezana did precisely as he was told to do.

After a moment, the lovebird said, "Now, turn around and open your eyes."

Ezana jerked his eyes open at the sound of the loud voice. To his surprise, the little bird transformed into a giant. He had never got so close to such an enormous animal in his life. He never expected that to happen, and he was scared to death in the dark.

"Don't freak out. It's me. Hop on my back," the lovebird said.

But the frightening voice didn't help Ezana. He needed more time to soothe himself. The lovebird tried to make him feel relaxed, but the more she spoke to him with her strange and loud voice, the scarier he became. Then she stopped talking and caressed him with her wings.

Finally, she calmed Ezana and helped him hop on her back. She made sure he sat comfortably and flew into the darkness like a flying dragon.

"This is how I took you home yesterday," she said in her loud voice.

Though still astonished by the entire experience, the more Ezana stayed safe in the air, the better and more relaxed he felt.

"This is insane!" he shouted.

"Not insane. This is so much sane," the lovebird said.

45

EZANA'S BIRTHDAY

On the morning of Ezana's birthday, his parents left their hotel room to celebrate his birthday at his grandparents' home. Ezana's grandma baked special Himbasha, and prepared sodas, milk, and yogurt. Until Ezana woke up, his parents and grandparents were engaged in conversation from Yared's childhood memories.

Ezana went to bed late around 3:00 A.M. the previous night. He was fascinated by the incredible experience he had with the lovebird. The exceptional ride home by the gigantic bird blew his mind. He couldn't go to sleep as soon as he got in bed. The reflection and analysis kept him awake for at least an hour. He liked to stay awake and reflect on the magical events so that he engraved them in his mind. He couldn't wait to go back to school in Denver and share his incredible experiences.

In the middle of stimulating conversation, Tsehay looked at her watch. "It's already 10:00 A.M. Let me wake Ezana up," she said and walked to the room he was sleeping in. She knocked several times before she entered, but he was in a deep sleep.

Tsehay started singing "Happy Birthday" to him. He smiled and struggled to open his eyes. She kissed him twelve times all over his face, one kiss for each year of his life. She helped him get up, dress up, and took him to the living room where everybody was waiting for the birthday boy. They all kissed him and wished him more blessings ahead.

Ezana's grandpa prayed and blessed the special Himbasha baked by his grandma. Then he cut the Himbasha into two halves on his only grandchild's back, according to the Tigrayan tradition. All clapped, smiled, and laughed in joy. The grandparents showered him with many blessings for more health, wealth, happiness, and success in life.

Ezana said, "Amen," for all the graces and graciously thanked his grandparents.

His parents gave him a wrapped birthday gift and waited anxiously for his reaction. Ezana unwrapped the present and discovered an ancient Aksumite cross. He remembered he saw the same crosses around the necks of the white brothers in the past.

Then to their surprise, his parents witnessed when his face lit up and glowed as if the cross projected a ray of light on his face. He hugged and kissed all of them one by one. His reaction took them by surprise. They thought the gift might be too small for his expectations, but he proved them wrong by embracing their gift happily. That threw their many days of worry out of the window.

His parents observed a remarkable change in their son, and they discussed it when Ezana left to take a shower. Tsehay and Yared agreed Ezana's grandparents did some magic to change him notably. And despite their refusal to take any credit for that, Tsehay and Yared praised them for their excellent job.

Ezana came out with his new ancient cross around his neck. His parents took him to swim at the Romhay Hotel, which Ezana appreciated so much. Although Ezana was appreciative and grateful for all of the efforts his parents made, his parents weren't sure that he was happy enough. Therefore, they searched for ice cream all over the city.

"Mom, you should start a pastry and ice cream business here," Ezana said.

"That's my dream, baby." She passionately explained how and what kind of delicious delicacies she would serve.

Finally, Yared found a place. One of the newly opened hotels had an ice cream parlor that served many flavors. Ezana ordered his favorite: vanilla.

After a series of lickings, Ezana said, "Yummy! Thank you, Mom, Dad, for everything."

"Are you sure you are happy, baby?" Tsehay asked, touched by him being considerate.

Ezana stopped licking for a moment and replied, "Totally, Mom."

"You were unhappy because you wanted to go to Disneyland for your birthday. That's why we are worried," Yared said.

Tsehay nodded her head up and down to strengthen what Yared said.

"I was, but now, I am cool about it. It's awesome," Ezana answered, smiling.

"And guess what?" Yared asked.

"What?"

"You tell him," Yared said to Tsehay.

Tsehay beamed in excitement and said, "I'll tell you later at dinner."

"Mom!" Ezana yelled, faking to be angry.

"Okay, okay. On our way back to Denver, we'll stop in LA for a couple of days, and we'll...take...you...to...Disney...land," she announced in Oprah Winfrey's voice.

Ezana shrugged his shoulders to indicate his lack of interest, which was the complete opposite of their anticipation.

"Ezana?" shouted his mom.

"What?" Ezana asked.

Tsehay couldn't believe it, and she gave her husband a "Can you believe this?" look.

"Does that mean you don't want to go to Disneyland anymore?" Yared asked.

"Please be cool. I know you are trying hard to make me happy. I'm grateful for that," Ezana replied, still working on his ice cream. "I am having fun already. But if you insist, we can go. It'll be the icing on the cake."

"Wow! I didn't know twelve was a magic number. Our boy is maturing," Tsehay said, caressing Ezana on the back and looking at Yared.

"Proud of you, son," Yared said.

On that night of Ezana's birthday, Tsehay and Yared wanted Ezana to spend the night with them at the hotel, but Ezana insisted that he liked to go back to his grandparents' house. After dinner, he gave goodnight hugs and kisses to his parents and left.

"Can you believe that?" Tsehay asked for the second time that day.

"Yes, our boy transformed into a confident young man at the age of twelve, and I'm proud of him," Yared replied, boastfully.

46

RIDING A GIANT

E zana set the alarm for 11:45 P.M. and went to bed early. He woke up by his body alarm clock before the alarm went off. He put some chocolates in the pocket of his sportswear and went out tiptoeing.

The lovebird waited for him at the usual time and place.

"I hope you didn't forget," the lovebird said sheepishly.

"Forget what?" Ezana asked.

"You know what."

"No, I don't."

"The chocolate. Hello!"

"Oh, the chocolate," Ezana said as if he didn't understand.

"So, did you bring me chocolate or not?" the lovebird asked eagerly.

"Yes, but I'll give it to you on one condition."

"Anything. Just do it fast, please."

"I want you to fly me like you did yesterday."

"You have got yourself a deal."

"I mean round trip flight," Ezana said.

"Sure."

The lovebird transformed into a gigantic being in the flat space between The Church of St. Mary of Zion and the stelae park. This time, Ezana witnessed the transformation with his eyes. He relished watching every moment of the process in astonishment. He was so amazed that he didn't notice the lovebird signaling him to hop on.

Flying high in the air again, it felt more like deja vu than real to Ezana. A full moon was above in the sky, radiating light all over the earth. The ride from takeoff to landing was short, but the lovebird did her best to make it longer and enjoyable. Ezana loved the bird's eye view down the outskirts of Aksum. He wished his friends in Denver, who were fans of fictional movies like How to Train Your Dragon, could see him fly a giant bird to an ancient African kingdom in the past.

They won't believe me, he thought, looking up to the sky and down to the earth.

The lovebird landed right at the gate of King Kaleb's ancient palace, which gave Ezana another chance to watch the bird shrinking back from gigantic to a tiny bird.

After the astonishing body and voice transformation of the lovebird took place, she chirped in her little voice, "Let's go visit some history."

The return of the tiny voice sounded funny to Ezana, and he held back his laughter. She didn't notice because she was busy enjoying her chocolate.

At 1:00 A.M, they entered into the time machine room and slipped down to the 4th century kingdom through the divine gate.

"Perfect timing," the lovebird said as soon as they landed in the past.

"What's going on?" Ezana asked, his eyes closed as he inhaled the fresh air of the 4th century.

"Let's go witness one of the most important milestones in the history of the Aksumite Kingdom."

47

A VICTORIOUS KING

After the enormous victory over the Kingdom of Meroe, the triumphant King Ezana came back to Aksum, leading his army. People of his kingdom and mothers, fathers, sons, and daughters of his soldiers all came out chanting to welcome him and his victorious army. Women ululated, men clapped, and children waved their hands for the king and his army. King Ezana jumped off his white horse, gracefully smiled and waved at the crowd, and shook the hands of some kids. Surrounded by his people, he walked down to the square of Aksum where a special ceremony was waiting.

He stepped up to a royal stage adorned by olive palms and guarded by lions and members of the monarch. The king caressed the lions with affection, and the lions cuddled to show their love to him. He kissed and hugged his mother and his twin brother. Then he greeted all of the noblemen, including the white brothers, and turned to the crowd and waved both hands with an enormous smile and pride. The people chanted his name until he gave them a sign to stop.

Then he delivered a speech of victory. He described how the heroic army of the Aksumite Kingdom destroyed the Kingdom of Meroe. The crowd applauded him by handclapping and ululating. Members of the royal family and noblemen gave him a standing ovation.

King Ezana concluded his speech saying, "The celebration and festivity of our victory will continue for days. May God bless you, my people."

The king traveled for many days but didn't show any signs of tiredness. He paced to a nearby park, followed by his family, noblemen, and the crowd. He ended the celebration of victory by inaugurating a statue of victory engraved with a trilingual inscription in Ge'ez, Sabean, and Greek. Ezana read the epigraphs and made sure that God was credited and praised enough for the victory over the Nubians and then approved and opened the statue of achievements for exhibition. His mentors, Frumentius and Edesius, gleamed with joy when they witnessed King Ezana attribute his great achievements to God.

48

A BOY MISSED

It was a rainy night in 21st-century Aksum, and a thunderbolt exploded and woke up the inhabitants of the city. Ezana's grandma got up and paced to Ezana's bedroom to check on him because she knew he liked to sleep with the window open. Guided by flashlight, she opened his room quietly and tiptoed to close the window. After she closed the leaking window, she realized Ezana wasn't in his bed. She checked for him in the bathroom, but he wasn't there.

She ran back into the living room and looked at the clock on the wall—it was 1:45 A.M. She was perplexed. She couldn't decide what to do. Finally, she decided to call her son. Yared didn't pick up. She dialed again and again, hoping the ring tone would wake him up.

"Hello," Yared replied in a trembling voice. "Mama, is everything all right?"

"Ezana—"

"What happened to him?" Yared asked, jumping off his bed.

"He's not in his bedroom," his mom said in her soft, sweet voice.

"I'm on my way," Yared said and hung up the phone.

"What do you mean he is not there?" Tsehay shouted when he woke her up and told her what happened.

Tsehay and Yared rushed out of their room with pajamas still on and went to the parking lot in the heavy rain. Both of them felt an overwhelming sense of dread and were unable to breathe or talk due to dry mouths. They didn't realize how heavy the rain was.

Ezana's parents and grandparents, relatives, neighbors, and police officers searched for Ezana. Many flashlights were used to search in every corner and sightseeing spot in the city. Tsehay cried every inch during the search. Yared, as worried as his wife, tried to comfort her all the way. Both wished Ezana had a local phone and regretted not getting him one. Residents of the city who woke up early to go to church joined them in the search after they learned about the unfortunate disappearance of the twelve-year-old boy.

49

THE KING SOLOMON OF AKSUM

M eanwhile, in the 4th century kingdom, Ezana and the lovebird continued attending the historical milestones of King Ezana in a phenomenal experience.

In the palace, King Ezana, Frumentius, and Edesius, started their discussion with a prayer.

"Praise to God," started the king. "With the help of God, our kingdom has become triumphant in all fronts. We are prospering in agriculture and trade. Our currency has become useful in many lands. People in our kingdom are living better and happier than ever. I believe great things are happening to us because God is with us."

The brothers' faces shone in happiness with every word the king uttered.

"God has honored me with his grace, and now, it's time for me to do something to honor him," the king added.

Tears of joy started to run down the brothers' faces. Both tried to hide their tears by wiping them with their clothes.

"My mother, my brother, and I have decided to build a church to worship God. We'll name the church St. Mary of Zion to honor the mother of our Lord, Jesus Christ. And we'll put the Ark of the Covenant in the church. What do you think?" the king asked.

Though the brothers' faces were shining with excitement, they were speechless. Edesius opened his mouth to speak, but no words came out.

Frumentius stumbled over a few words. "Your Majesty, God really and truly blessed you. You're the chosen one like Solomon. We served your father too, but God waited for you to build him His house as He waited for King Solomon..." Frumentius couldn't go on. Tears of emotion interrupted.

"I'm honored to hear all that. I'm grateful for you introducing us to the faith of Christianity and our Lord, Jesus Christ. On behalf of my family and my kingdom, I would like to thank you for all your kind services. Now, it's time for us to let you go to your family and land. You can come back anytime you wish. Sunday night, we'll have a farewell dinner in the palace garden. You can invite the guests you would like to attend," King Ezana said.

The brothers welcomed the great news in a whirl of delight. They were out of words, so they expressed their happiness in their tears of joy. The king and the brothers stood for prayers before parting ways.

"How about a walk in the park listening to the rest on audio?" the lovebird whispered to Ezana.

He agreed and exited from the fabulous palace. When they got outside, they saw noblemen, wise men, architects, merchants, and artisans coming toward the chamber, and the lovebird remembered something.

"You are no longer interested in the comedy, I think?" she asked.

"Oh! I was supposed to work on it yesterday, but after the mind-blowing ride, I forgot everything. Who could think of something other than that unbelievable ride anyway?"

The lovebird shook her head. She wanted him to enjoy the experience of performing on the 4th-century stage for an ancient audience.

"So, are you interested in giving it a try?"

"A million percent!" he exclaimed.

"Great. Let's go check the next program," the lovebird said and chirped something to put the audio narration on.

Ezana startled like the first day when he heard the golden voice of the narrator.

50

REVEALER OF LIGHT

T he great king of the Aksumite Kingdom, King Ezana, achieved much in agriculture, war, construction, and trade after he became the first king of the kingdom to embrace Christianity. The king attributed his successes to God, and he honored God by minting the sign of the cross on the coins of his kingdom.

Aksum became the first state ever to use the image of the cross on its currency.

When the king hosted a welfare dinner for the white brothers, he promised the brothers that he would build the first church in the kingdom. Accordingly, the next day after the brothers left Aksum, Ezana assembled his master builders and designers, who erected the magnificent Stela of Ezana. He ordered them to bring him a design for The Church of St. Mary of Zion, and he appointed his brother, Saizana, to command the project of the church.

Meanwhile, the white brothers left for their land, Tyre. Frumentius detoured to Alexandria to ask the patriarch of Alexandria to send a bishop to Aksum.

A couple of months later, in Aksum, the master builders of the kingdom submitted an elegant design for the future house of God. Ezana and Saizana, along with their mother, Queen Sophia, sat to approve the blueprint and allocate land for the building.

Frumentius walked in as the first bishop of Aksum, anointed by Athanasius, patriarch of the Church of Alexandria. The king and his family *were surprised and pleased to have him back. Frumentius explained how he asked the patriarch of Alexandria to send a bishop.*

However, the Patriarch insisted on anointing him instead and sent him back. The monarch cherished what he told them and took it as a miracle from God. Frumentius, the new bishop of Aksum, joined the royal family in approving the blueprint and launch of the construction of the church.

Bishop Frumentius officially baptized the king and his family and the entire kingdom into Christianity. The monarch allowed Frumentius to build many churches in the kingdom after the first church, The Church of St. Mary of Zion, in Aksum. He traveled throughout the country to evangelize. People adoringly called him Abba Selama Kesate Birhan, which meant Revealer of Light.

The Aksumite Kingdom became the second official Christian state in the world, following Armenia's lead roughly twenty-five years after the Eastern European country adopted the faith.

51

DANCING AROUND DANGER: COMEDY SHOW

The lovebird stopped the audio narration when they arrived at the amphitheater in the palace.

"A heartwarming and inspiring history. Thank you, bird," Ezana said.

"Praise the Lord! I'm glad you loved it. Now let's work to put you on the stage." She flew around the amphitheater, the stage, and the room behind. Ezana started thinking of his favorite comedians to borrow their hilarious jokes.

"Who is relatable?" Ezana murmured.

"Relatable to what?" the lovebird asked, landing on Ezana's shoulder.

"I'm thinking about comedians who can relate to the ancient audience," Ezana said, still running through the top comedians of the 21st century in his mind.

"Well, it seems there wasn't any show in here since the coronation of King Ezana," she said in a soft voice.

Ezana looked at her with wide eyes. He thought he lost the chance to perform in front of the ancient audience, and suddenly, he wanted it badly.

"I hope you are not telling me there is no chance. I am sure there is a possibility, right?"

The lovebird closed her eyes to do some thinking. Ezana waited for her reply, which he didn't get. He grabbed and moved her from his shoulder to his face and saw what she was doing.

"There is one, but it comes with a challenge," the lovebird said with her eyes still closed.

Ezana waited for clarification.

"The late King Ella Amida's friend has a similar fancy in comedy." She opened her eyes. "He lives in Adulis. He's the mayor of the port city."

"That sounds great. We can use the divine gate, right?" Ezana asked excitedly.

"Yes, but there is one problem."

"Problem? I just heard this word for the first time since I met you."

"Hahaha. Good one. The mayor gives gold, jewelry, and ivory to the funny ones," the lovebird said.

"That's not what we would call a problem. In my world, we call that a prize," Ezana said.

"Here is the problem. The mayor throws the unfunny ones into the mouths of his lions."

Ezana stepped back in shock. "Why would he do that?"

The way he reacted made the lovebird explode into her fancy laughter.

"If he can't laugh at your jokes, he laughs on your screaming to death," the lovebird said, struggling with her laughter. "The great thing though is if you make him laugh, you will be laughing all the way to the bank with expensive gifts of ivory and jewelry."

Ezana imagined the mayor laughing like crazy, watching his lions eating the bombed and booed comedians. Ezana felt adrenaline rush through his veins.

"You seem worried. Forget it. Let's go home," the lovebird said and jumped back on his shoulder.

"It's both frightening and exhilarating at the same time. Plus, I know so many killer jokes, and making the audience of the ancient world laugh will be super easy. It's gonna be fun." Ezana started walking away from the amphitheater.

"I can't wait to see you on the stage. It's going to be fun," the lovebird said, fired up.

On the way out, they bumped into the king and foreign delegates. Ezana observed the diversity in the group of people surrounding the king and became curious. He asked the bird why did so many people came from all over the world. The lovebird proudly reminded him that the Aksumite Kingdom was one of the four ancient civilizations to ever flourished on the globe, and many nations had different levels of interest in staying in touch with Aksum.

"By the way, this might be our final visit," the lovebird said right after they left the palace compound.

Ezana ceased walking. "What about the comedy stage?"

"Oh, good to know you are seriously into it. Then that will be the climax of the experience," the lovebird said.

52

FROM MONARCHS TO SAINTS

When back from the past, Ezana asked the lovebird how King Ezana and his brother ended up in the history of Aksum.

"King Ezana and Saizana changed their names to Abreha and Atsbeha and then left the monarchy to commit themselves to God. They spent the rest of their lives building churches around the country.

For their outstanding services to God and the church of the kingdom, they were anointed as saints. They finally rested in the church Abreha & Atsbeha that was dedicated to them," the lovebird said.

The name Abreha & Atsbeha rang a bell to Ezana, and he remembered visiting the church with his parents. He regretted the fact that he had no interest in anything back then.

"How about we end the night deliciously?" the bird asked sheepishly while stepping out of King Kaleb's palace underground.

"Haha...let me check if I have some left," Ezana sent his hand into his pocket to fetch a bar of chocolate.

53

THE STORY THAT SHOCKED EZANA'S PARENTS

In present day Aksum, the search for Ezana continued until the first light in the morning, but he was nowhere to find. Police examined Ezana's bedroom, but no indications of any criminal activity were found. Then the police interviewed both of his parents and grandparents in his office, at the police station. Still, they couldn't find any clue that led them to discover Ezana or reach a conclusion.

The officer kept repeating that the city never had such an experience.

"Are you sure nobody has gone missing before?" Yared asked the policeman.

The policeman opened his mouth but paused. Yared and Tsehay, their eyes and mouth wide opened, waited, hoping he would say something. The policeman changed his mind. He sighed heavily instead.

"Please don't hold it back, officer. It doesn't matter whether it's good or bad. Just tell us the truth," Tsehay insisted.

"It happened a long time ago. There was a five-year-old missing child reported," he said and got up to escort them out.

"Wait, officer. What happened to the missing child?" Tsehay asked.

The police officer sank back in his chair. "Somebody abducted and sold the boy. And the buyer used him as a prop for begging."

Yared was aware of such cases, but Tsehay wasn't. She looked at the policeman, horrified. Yared knew his wife would freak out, and he wished the policeman didn't go into that story. He sliced a finger across his throat as to say, "Cut it," to the policeman. The policeman stood again, but Tsehay gave him a look for "Where do you think you are going?" without finishing the story.

"Then?" Tsehay asked, gazing at him unbelievably.

"The police found the boy after two years," the policeman said, head down in shame.

"Two years?" Tsehay exploded.

"The man who bought him for begging purpose was taking him all over the country, and it was difficult to track him down," he said apologetically.

Every word that came out from the policeman gave Tsehay cold chills and terrified her. The policeman attempted to stand up and see them out, but Tsehay asked him how they found the boy.

"I was hoping you wouldn't ask me that," he said and rested both elbows on the table. "His mother searched all over the country since the boy went missing. One lucky day in *Addis Ababa*, while she was in a taxi, saw her abducted boy guiding a blind beggar at the street's traffic light. She screamed, made the taxi stop in the middle of traffic, and was reunited with her child after two years."

Tsehay slowly stood up and started walking out, heartbroken.

"Don't worry. Nothing will be out of hand. We'll take care of the situation," the policeman said and begged the family to get some rest.

Yared knew the policeman was desperate, but the family needed to hear such kind words from the police.

After long hours of searching and the interview with the police, they all were on the way home exhausted and shivering cold. The grandparents went to church to pray for Ezana's safe return. Yared enfolded his tired, shaking, and crying wife and walked back to his parents' house.

As soon as they got back, Tsehay collapsed in the living room. Yared insisted she take some rest in bed, but she refused to do so. Then he walked into Ezana's bedroom to bring her a blanket. When he entered the room where he spent his childhood, he couldn't believe what his eyes showed him. Ezana was in bed asleep peacefully. It felt like deja vu to him, and he closed and opened his eyes to make sure what he saw was real. He got closer to his son, touched him, felt his breath, and ran back to the living room.

"Honey, he's back!" Yared shouted. "Ezana is back. He's in his bed."

Tsehay got up and sprinted to the bedroom like a hundred-meter dash athlete. She almost knocked her husband down on her way to the bedroom. She jumped into the bed and squeezed Ezana. She kissed him a million times. He was in a deep sleep, and she didn't wake him up with all her energy of love and excitement.

Yared watched her reaction from behind like a dazzling performance, and tears of joy ran all over his face.

"Honey, I got to go tell everybody the great news."

"Okay, hun!" she shouted back without paying attention to what he said.

54

TSEHAY'S CONFESSION

After she realized Ezana's safe return home was real, Tsehay started to worry about the fact that he couldn't wake up, although she did many things that should have woken him up. She took off his blanket and opened the window to let some fresh air get in. Unconsciously, she went back to the kitchen to make breakfast for Ezana and coffee for herself. She heard him waking up from the next room in the kitchen, and she served him breakfast in bed.

"Good morning, sunshine! Himbasha, honey, and milk. Simple breakfast the way you like it," Tsehay said, wearing a broad smile all over.

"Mom, what are you doing here this early?" Ezana asked, still dizzy.

"Well, we have a lot to talk about, but eat your breakfast first." She put more pillows behind his back and pushed a breakfast tray to his chest.

"It's so early, Mom." He pushed the tray away, pulled the blanket back up, and covered himself.

She uncovered him jokingly and managed to wake him up, but he wasn't ready to eat. He grabbed the hot milk and pushed back the rest. After sipping the hot cow milk, Ezana noticed his mom not only came over early but was also in pajamas. He thought something wrong might have happened between her and his dad.

Tsehay took back the breakfast tray to the kitchen and sat comfortably beside Ezana on the bed, cleared her throat, and gazed intently into his eyes.

"Mom, what is it? Is everything all right with you and Dad?"

"Everything is all right, my baby..." She burst into tears

Ezana hugged and soothed her.

"Baby, I have a confession to make. You know, that car accident that took my father's life left me devastated. I was depressed. I couldn't recover for a long time. I wasn't a good mom to you, and I wasn't good wife to your dad..." She sobbed.

"No, Mom. What are you talking about?" He hugged her. "You're the best Mom on the planet," he whispered in her ear.

She felt his sweet words rushed through her system and made her glow and smile. She squeezed and kissed him.

"Your dad planned this trip to heal me from grief. I was selfish. And guiltiness is killing me, baby. We should have taken you to Disneyland, not put your birthday on the side. I'm so sorry, my baby. I'll make it up to you." She exploded into tears again.

Ezana couldn't understand why his mom was on such an emotional rollercoaster. Still, he kept doing his best to calm her down.

"Mom, I don't understand why you are feeling bad about this trip. I loved it. I don't know if it worked for you and healed you, but it worked perfectly fine for me. The most awesome birthday I have ever have."

"Are you sure about that?" Tsehay pushed Ezana away with both hands to see him eye to eye.

"A million percent, Mom. This is an awesome trip," he said with a sparkling face.

Yared came back after informing his parents at the church, everyone who joined them in the search and reported to the police.

Tsehay cleaned her tears by her cloth as soon as he walked in, which he didn't miss noticing.

"It must be tears of joy," Yared said, smiling joyfully and kissing both of them.

"Thank God! Can I go to sleep now? Please," Ezana begged.

"Okay, let's go to the hotel. We all need some sleep," Yared said.

"Dad, but I'm so dozy. Let me sleep here."

"No, get up and get dressed, baby. There is no way we leave you here," Tsehay said in a sharp tone that Ezana knew he shouldn't challenge.

When Ezana threw the blanket away and started to get up, Tsehay and Yared went to the living room. Yared asked her if she talked to him about the puzzling disappearance.

"You just walked in when I was about to get into that point."

"Okay, we'll talk to him later after he wakes up," Yared said, feeling good that he didn't miss anything.

They all went to sleep at the Yeha Hotel. Tsehay couldn't sleep. She tossed in bed until her family woke up. She tried to solve the puzzle behind Ezana's disappearance, but she couldn't reach anything convincing. So, she got up and took a long meditating shower, which made her feel grateful for the life she lived.

When Yared and Ezana woke up, they didn't find the Tsehay they saw before they went to bed. Her sense of optimism was terrific. She was dancing to her favorite R&B songs from the '90s, cheerfully.

"My wife is back!" Yared shouted.

She didn't hear him. Tsehay unplugged her earphones and scrolled her phone.

"I was searching for a new restaurant we haven't tried, and I found an interesting one. TripAdvisor gave it four and a half stars with good reviews. Let's check it out," she suggested, looking at both with her gleaming eyes.

They both agreed.

55

THE EXORCISM

They arrived at the four-and-a-half-star restaurant in fifteen minutes. It had clean parking lot and beautiful garden at the front, and a guy welcomed them with a big smile at the gate.

"I give it two stars already," Tsehay said.

"So far so good!" Yared replied.

Usually, when Yared and Tsehay went to restaurants, it was not always about the food and drinks but more about the experience. The smiles and follow-ups by waiters, the cleanliness of the restrooms, and the amiability of the environment mattered the most to them. To their surprise, this restaurant checked all of the boxes. They were eager to taste the food and ordered a three-course meal. They ate silently—Ezana had not eaten for many hours, and Tsehay and Yared were still preoccupied with what exactly happened to Ezana.

"Delicious dishes," Tsehay finally said, breaking the silence.

"Yes. First, I thought it tasted delicious only because I was starving. But I'm wrong," Yared said, mouthful.

"How is your food, baby?" Tsehay asked Ezana.

"Awesome."

"I think this restaurant deserves five stars. What do you guys think?" Tsehay wanted to keep the conversation rolling.

"I agree," Yared said, holding all five fingers up.

"I'll tell you after the dessert," Ezana said, smiling.

For a dessert, Tsehay had Tiramisu, Ezana had chocolate cake, and Yared skipped the pastry and went for black coffee.

Ezana gave it two thumbs up and agreed with his mom on the five-star suggestion.

The three-course meal was enjoyed thoroughly. Everybody left the restaurant, and the three of them remained alone in the restaurant. The time and place couldn't be more perfect for questioning Ezana. Tsehay and Yared communicated with their eyes. Ezana didn't have any idea about what was coming, so he was acting normal, even happier than before.

"Ezana, where were you yesterday?" Yared asked.

Ezana froze with an open mouth for a moment and stumbled over meaningless words.

"It's okay, baby. Tell us what happened." His mother caressed him on his back in a sense of encouragement.

"What do you mean?" Ezana asked while trying to figure out what to tell them.

"Ezana, your mom and I, your grandparents, many other very kind people, and members of the city police spent many hours outside during the heavy rain last night searching for you," Yared said in a firmer tone than earlier.

"Your grandma called us after midnight when she couldn't find you anywhere in the house?" Tsehay said in a softer voice.

"I'm sorry I caused you trouble." Ezana put his head down, and his foot started hitting the ground unconsciously.

"Apology accepted. But you didn't answer the question. Where were you?" Yared asked impatiently.

Ezana hesitated to answer, still working to form a believable story.

Although his mom kept encouraging him to feel free to tell them whatever happened, the temper of his dad scared Ezana.

Tsehay intervened and calmed her husband. Yared called a waitress and ordered another cup of coffee in an effort to ease himself.

"I was with a friend," Ezana said.

"A friend? Who's your friend? And where were you, and what were you doing at such a time?" Yared asked quickly.

Ezana never expected that would happen and didn't prepare himself for it. He just sat, putting on his most angelic face.

"Come on, baby. Tell us everything," Tsehay said, begging him to speak up.

"I was with a good friend in a safe place having fun, all right?"

Yared became impatient. He stood up and then sat again. Tsehay touched him on his lap to calm him down.

"Go ahead, baby. Who is your good friend, and where were you?" Tsehay asked.

"You won't believe me, so I better not tell you the details."

Yared sipped the remaining coffee in his cup, leaned toward Ezana, and started to talk in a low voice, which terrified Ezana more than the louder voice.

"Listen to me, boy. This is not a joke. It's not only about us. The police also need a detailed report. If you don't want to tell us, then I'll take you to the police station." Yared leaned back.

"And you won't like the way the police interrogate," Tsehay suggested.

Ezana remembered the story about the American girl and the Nigerian police. He didn't want to go through the African kind of discipline.

He burst into sobbing and opened up. He told them everything, how he met the lovebird, the night visits to the magical world, and how the bird took him through a divine gate located in the palace of King Kaleb.

In the middle of the story, Ezana thought his parents were interested in his story and became excited. He explained how his friend, the lovebird, loved chocolate and how her entire body smiled when he gave her a bar of chocolate. He concluded his unusual story illustrating how the bird transformed into a gigantic being to carry him to and from the palace.

"Oh, god. I think a demon-possessed our baby," Tsehay whispered to her husband and exploded into tears.

"It sounds like that. I'll tell my parents to take him to the church for prayers and exorcism," Yared whispered back into his wife's ear while comforting her on his chest.

"I knew it. I told you that you wouldn't believe me," Ezana said in frustration.

Tsehay moved from her husband to Ezana, and she pulled him in and embraced him tightly.

Yared drove his wife and son to the hotel and went to meet his parents. Ezana wanted to go back to his grandpa's so that he could avoid the awkward moment and also exercise the freedom to spend more time with the lovebird. But both Yared and Tsehay rejected the idea.

Yared explained to his parents the story behind Ezana's disappearance. Yared's parents listened to him quietly. They didn't overreact to the story as he expected. Their usual tranquility didn't change.

After he told the story intensely, using his whole body, he sat down and sighed.

"Take it easy, son," said his father. "Let's take him for holy water bathing in Our Lady Mary of Zion for three days."

His mom nodded her head to agree with what her husband said.

"Well, that's what I thought," Yared replied. "We must extend our stay. I'll bring Ezana to the church early in the morning,"

Yared would have felt better if his parents looked at the matter with the same urgency as he did. They simply suggested the holy water bathing and got back to their prayer routines.

56

ACTING NORMAL

Back at the hotel, Ezana wanted to reassure his mom that everything was all right with him. He engaged her with stimulating conversation.

"Mom, so did it work out?"

"What work out, baby?" asked Tsehay, opening up for the conversation.

"You said Dad planned this trip to heal you from depression."

"Oh, yes, it worked perfectly. I promise I'll be a great mom and wife."

"You have always been great, Mom, but I am super glad to hear that."

Tsehay jumped to his bed, lay next to him, and stared at him with compassion. "You know how much your dad and I love you, right?"

"No doubt, Mom. And I love you both more."

"We are just worried about you, baby."

"I know and am so sorry. I wish I knew what to do to make you feel better."

She started caressing his hair. "You can tell us the truth, baby."

Ezana jumped down from the bed. "If you want to know the truth, let's go outside meet the bird," said Ezana confidently, walking outside.

She hoped he was back to his senses, and she felt her heart sink when he mentioned the bird again. She followed him outside out of sympathy.

***

At the spot outside at the Yeha Hotel, which Ezana and the bird agreed to name "The Best View in Aksum," Ezana stood next to his mother, hoping the bird would come. He gazed at the sky with eagerness like never before. His mom ashamedly looked at the direction her son fixed his eyes. Usually, the lovebird appeared as soon as Ezana looked out for her, but this time, she didn't show up when he wanted her badly.

"Mom, let's sit and wait. She will come for sure," Ezana encouraged her.

Tsehay did what he said just to make him happy. Both of them sat under the porch of the glassed restaurant. When a waitress came and engaged Tsehay, Ezana walked to the spot and paced back and forth, talking to himself. "Dear bird, please come. Please come."

When Tsehay saw him talking with himself and moving around like that, she started to feel pain, and she drowned in fear.

"Oh my, baby, what happened to you?" she muttered to herself.

After eagerly pacing back and forth, Ezana gave up and sat next to his mom.

Suddenly, he stood up and shouted, "Bird!" pointing his finger to the sky. He jumped up and down in excitement. Tsehay looked up toward where he pointed his finger, but she couldn't see anything.

"Mom, did you see her? My friend, the bird, is here!" he shouted.

"Where is it? I couldn't see it," she said in a sad voice.

"Wait for a minute, Mom," Ezana said. "Hey, lovebird, come a little closer. Come down to meet my mom!"

The lovebird looked down, saw what was going on, turned back, and flew away.

"Oh, no! Come on, bird!" Ezana roared.

Tsehay wiped her tears with her scarf. "Baby, let's go to our room."

"I'm sorry, Mom. The bird isn't in a good mood today."

***

Back in the hotel room, Tsehay went to take a shower, which meant to cry inside the bathroom.

Ezana reflected on what happened outside. Why couldn't his mom see the bird while he could see her? He ran the entire episode through in his mind, and he realized the bird made him look like a lunatic.

"Or am I losing my mind? Is it all a dream or some illusion?" he asked himself. "But I experienced the miracle not once, not twice, but plenty of times!"

He accepted right there and then that his mom had every right to be worried after watching that drama with the bird. Then he decided to act like a regular kid from Denver, and he pulled out his tablet, switched it on, and connected to the WiFi. When Yared walked in from outside and Tsehay from the bathroom, Ezana was lying on the bed, playing games. And that old habit gave them hope.

After a long sleepless night and day, Yared complained about a headache and asked Tsehay if she wanted to join him for coffee.

"I would love to. I'm feeling drowsy myself."

Yared cruised by Ezana's bed and informed him they are going out for coffee. "You can join us if you want something," he offered.

Ezana showed him the game he was playing. "I'd like to stay here and play the game. Thanks though, Dad," Ezana said adorably. "Besides..." He halted himself from finishing the line.

"Besides?" Yared asked.

"Never mind, Dad."

"Are you sure you don't want anything?"

"A million percent, Dad."

Tsehay and Yared stepped out.

"Besides...I know you want to talk about me," Ezana finished the line.

Tsehay and Yared favored the coffee bar in the hotel to take the chance to talk about their son's circumstance. Yared started the conversation by updating Tsehay about his visit to his parents and their decision to take Ezana to church for a three-day bathing in holy water.

"That's a good decision," Tsehay said and refrained from telling him what happened earlier between Ezana and his imaginary friend, the bird. But she changed her mind after he drank two cups of coffee in a row and was relieved from the headache. She tried to illustrate to him what happened as smoothly as possible so that he wouldn't freak out, which she regretted in thirty seconds. Yared exploded into tears. He couldn't handle it.

Ezana knew they would be talking about him. He also suspected his mom might tell his dad what happened. He stopped the game and started thinking about how to handle the situation to make them less concerned.

"What is the coolest thing that I can do to make them think I didn't lose my mind?" he asked himself and waited for an answer.

What the bird once said about him echoed in his head: "You are smart, you know." He put his tablet away, stood up, and wandered in the suit room to figure out something smart that could make him look like a regular kid.

He picked up his tablet and Googled, what do regular twelve-year-old kids do?

Nothing that satisfied or interested him came up. He threw back the tablet on the couch and kept rambling inside the room. Something popped up in his head, and suddenly, he stopped pacing in the room. *They think some evil spirit possessed me. So, I have to act opposite to that.* His face beamed in a eureka moment.

Half an hour later, Tsehay and Yared got back to their room in a melancholier mood than when they left. When Yared was about to put a key into the keyhole, he heard Gospel music coming out from their room. He couldn't believe that sound came from their hotel room. He rested his ear on the door to make sure and gave Tsehay the face for

"Can you believe this?" Tsehay did the same to listen, and her whole body changed from blue to lively. Yared's body mirrored Tsehay's cheerfulness.

They both liked to listen to Gospel songs and tried to pass on that habit to Ezana, but he instead kept on listening to his favorite music of hip hop, rock, and pop music. Now, all of a sudden, he played some of the Christian Mezmur, which wonderfully surprised them.

Yared turned the key and pushed open the door quietly. They both tiptoed into the room. Ezana was asleep on the bed, over the coverlet. Tsehay put a blanket on him. Yared picked up Ezana's tablet to see what was playing, which was Christian Mezmur mix on YouTube.

Tsehay and Yared smiled at each other. Then they met in the middle of the room to share a kiss of relief. Ezana's plan worked out perfectly.

57

FIRST RITE OF EXORCISM

Early in the Aksum morning, Yared and Tsehay took Ezana to The Church of St. Mary of Zion. Ezana didn't complain about waking up early as he used to do, which earned him another good point from his parents.

When they arrived at the church, Ezana's grandparents were already there waiting. Before they went straight down to the chapel where the exorcism healing takes place, Yared and Tsehay walked to the main church to pray. When they reached a stone marker, they separated and went down different pathways to the men's and women's gates. Ezana followed his dad to the men's entrance of the church.

The chapel where patients and demon-possessed people visit for spiritual healing stood away from the principal church. A priest with a cross on hand and holy water perform evicting demons or other spiritual entities from people.

It was so early. Ezana arrived first escorted by his parents and grandparents at the place. The priest exchanged greetings with Ezana's grandparents. He let them all kiss his hand cross and blessed each one of them.

Without asking for any explanation, the priest held Ezana's hand so tight and vanished into another room behind a curtain. Yared thought his parents must have informed the priest beforehand. Ezana undressed and got into the bath happily. The priest applauded him and showered him not only with the holy water but also with blessings.

Customarily, when someone was possessed by demons, he or she started to scream and shout as soon as he or she felt the holy water. Then the priest forced the evil spirit to leave the patient in the name of Jesus Christ using the cross and holy water. Ezana's parents expected something similar. However, Ezana only showed a sensitivity reaction to the freezing holy water that descended from a high, wide-open hose and hit him hard. Otherwise, he finished the healing bath gracefully, which got him another good point in proving him to be a normal kid.

Back in the hotel, Ezana continued to be pretty decent and well. That made his parents relaxed. They ate lunch in the hotel's restaurant. After lunch, they went back to their hotel room and stayed inside.

The hotel room turned into a luxury library. His parents took advantage of the well-being of their son to read books for the rest of the afternoon. Tsehay opened Elizabeth Gilbert's Eat Pray Love in the middle, guided by a bookmark. Yared started one of the books he got for the trip—John Grisham's Rogue Lawyer.

Ezana tired of playing games and mimicked his parents. He laid down on the couch of the living room of the suite room with a comic book written by his favorite comic writer, Stan Lee. All of a sudden, Ezana's reading interest died in the middle of his favorite book. The lovebird kept coming up in his imagination, but he ignored her and focus on reading. He fought the temptation to go outside to look for her because he knew that his parents wouldn't let him go alone.

"Stay cool. Build trust today so that they can trust you tomorrow," Ezana whispered to himself.

But again, the bird started to fly across the comic book. Ezana folded the comic, placed it on his chest, and stared at the ceiling, which appeared convenient for the lovebird to fly on. Then he closed his eyes, but that didn't help. He tried to avoid her from his imagination, but she came through his ears.

"Why are you confined in this room?" the lovebird asked him mockingly.

"Please go away!" Ezana replied, his eyes closed.

Those little three words Ezana murmured jolted Yared and Tsehay at the same time.

"Ezu, are you okay?"

"Yes, I'm okay," Ezana replied.

"You said something?"

"No, Dad."

"You said, 'Please go away.'"

Ezana didn't know he said those words out loud and became mad at himself for losing a point.

His mom jumped down from the bed and paced toward him. "It's all right, baby. It's all right. You must have been dreaming," she said, trying to encourage him.

He thought that was a good idea, and he acted like it. He closed his eyes.

Those words ruined the tranquility of the room. Yared and Tsehay put their books down and went back to being worrisome. Ezana did well the whole day, and he almost regained his parents' confidence.

But then ruined it at the eleventh hour. He wanted to fix it. When he began planning his next move, his parents' discussion attracted his attention. He overheard them talking about him in pity.

"If he's not getting well after the three-day holy water bathing, we should extend our stay so that he can get the seven-day rite," said Yared in a concerned tone.

Tsehay nodded in agreement while trying to control her tears.

Ezana felt guilty for causing his parents such trouble. With caution not to let words slip again, Ezana began planning to destroy the doubt his parents held over him, and he fell asleep while contemplating.

58

SECOND RITE OF EXORCISM

Ezana's second day at the church was similar to the first day. His parents woke him up early in the morning and took him down to the church. The three of them prayed. They were joined by Ezana's grandparents and went to the holy water bathing chapel.

A girl and her parents arrived at the sacred water bathing before them. The girl screamed and cried during the rites. That bothered Ezana. It was a cold morning as the previous day, and he felt butterflies in his stomach when he thought about the freezing holy water. But he planned it to be flawless to regain his parents' trust.

Once I get their trust, I'll go out to meet the lovebird and arrange the comedy performance, he thought.

Tsehay apologized and went back to the main hall of the church to continue the prayer. The girl came out with her family, trembling to death. Ezana couldn't tell if she screamed due to the freezing holy water or from an evil spirit. The priest called for the next patient in line.

Ezana stood up and went before his dad gave him the signal. Usually, a demon-possessed person resisted going into the holy water. Ezana heard his grandparents talk about it. He wanted to milk any situation to disprove the notion of him being possessed by evil.

While Ezana was undressing, he saw Yared whispering something to the priest. The whisper came to light as the priest became more aggressive on him than the previous day. Ezana didn't scream or shout.

178

His toughest challenge was the extreme coldness of the sacred water.

On their way back to the hotel, Ezana fell asleep. Tsehay asked Yared if there was anything new.

"Nothing," he replied.

Tsehay remained silent.

"I am supposed to be happy about it. But for a reason I don't understand, part of me wanted to see something different," Yared said. "How do you explain that?" he asked Tsehay.

"I felt the same. I guess it's because we were convinced something was wrong, and we wanted that healed," Tsehay explained.

As planned, Ezana stayed in the hotel room all day. His parents asked him to go out for lunch and dinner, but he declined. Yared and Tsehay stayed inside with him, mostly reading. He slept, played games, and read his comic books. He was in charge of ordering food and drinks from room service too. No tears shed. Instead, they had moments of laughter.

Ezana nailed the day without any blunder.

59

THIRD RITE OF EXORCISM

The third day at the church went well. After Ezana was baptized in holy water and dressed up, his grandparents escorted him out of the baptizing chapel and into the car in the parking lot. His parents stayed behind to speak to the priest in private on what to do next.

The priest apologized to his next patient in line and joined Tsehay and Yared, who still looked worried about their son's health. The priest sent his hand into his pocket for his blessing cross, but it wasn't there.

He realized he forgot the cross behind in the baptizing room, and he apologized with a shy smile. Tsehay encouraged him to let them kiss his hand, and he gave them his right hand to save time. They both kissed his hand and received his prayers.

"I understand you're worried," the priest said. "Don't worry. Your son is healthy, blessed by God."

Tsehay's and Yared's faces glowed at the same time.

"Keep taking him to church often," the priest suggested. "May God bless your health, your family, and your marriage."

"Amen, Father," Tsehay said.

"Amen, and thank you so much, Father," Yared added.

The priest lit them up with the good news and blessings. They walked to the car where Ezana was waiting for them.

"Oh! I feel relieved," Tsehay said.

"Same here," Yared added.

Ezana saw them through the car window, coming with huge smiles on their faces. When his parents got into the car, Ezana acted asleep with a smile on his face. Yared started the engine, and Tsehay turned around to the back seat to check on Ezana.

"Oh, my baby! He's sleeping with a beautiful smile on his face. How wonderful," she said.

"That's great," Yared said and looked at his boy quickly. He turned back to the steering wheel and checked the watch on the dashboard.

"It's time. What do you want to eat for breakfast?" Yared asked.

60

KINDNESS IS A LANGUAGE

Tsehay and Yared were a community-oriented couple. They participated in community services and donations both in Tigray and the United States. On this tour, they both brought many books for local schools.

Yared drove directly to a school located in the center city of Aksum where he attended his elementary classes. One of his old teachers, now a principal of the school, alongside a few younger teachers and several young students, waited for them and gave them a warm welcome. The students dressed up in clean school uniforms sang the national anthem, Zeyndybo Gobo, for the guests' honor.

Ezana was dazzled by their impressive welcoming ceremony. After the children performed the anthem passionately, Yared handed seventy-five books to the school principal. He collected those books over the years for the elementary school.

"As Mark Twain said, kindness is the language which the deaf can hear, and the blind can see," the principal said. "Not only have we received the book donation, but we have also learned kindness." He concluded his brief speech and gave them an exclusive tour of the school, including the classes Yared sat in for years.

In the end, a traditional coffee ceremony with himbasha and honey was served. The old teachers blessed Yared and his family for their generous contributions. The hospitality of the school community touched the hearts of the family from Denver. Ezana witnessed how the teachers and the students loved and valued the book donations. He regretted not attending when his mom donated her books in Mekelle.

I was a complete jerk back then, Ezana confessed. The idea of being a jerk reminded him of Luwam. *Wow! How changed I am in just a few days!*

"I'm sorry I didn't attend your ceremony, Mom," he whispered to Tsehay.

"Oh! It's okay, baby. It was pretty much the same," she said, pressing her hand on her chest to express how touched she was.

Ezana promised to himself to follow his parents' good example and bring his comic books on his next trip. And the idea of planning to come back gave him a feeling of delight because the lovebird promised him more surprising adventures in the coming summer.

After the book donation program ended, the teachers and students escorted them to their car parked outside the school compound.

When Yared started driving away from his childhood school, Ezana asked Tsehay to call her sister in Mekelle and put her daughter, Luwam, on for him. Tsehay was delighted to hear his request, and she did what he asked with pleasure. Ezana asked Luwam to forgive him for being a jerk to her. Luwam accepted his apology after teasing him for a while. He hung up the phone and breathed a sigh of relief. His parents listened attentively to his phone conversation with Luwam, and they believed that their boy was not only healthy but also kinder than the week before. Both lit up and praised him for his courage to apologize.

It was one of the most beautiful days of their vacation—until late in the afternoon. After lunch, they cruised in the city shopping for some souvenirs, traditional handcrafts, and the distinguished honey of Tigray. The shopping chore alerted Ezana that they would be leaving Aksum soon, and he started to think about the lovebird. He wanted to meet her and didn't want to miss the chance to do the comedy performance in the 4th-century stage.

61

EZANA'S SECRET WEAPON

When they got back to the hotel, Ezana helped his parents unload the stuff they bought to take to Denver as memorabilia and gifts for friends. The sweat he got from helping gave him another reason to take a shower. In the shower, he kept thinking about how to go outside to meet his friend without creating any drama.

You read a book while they do the packing and unpacking stuff. Then you get some sleep, or at least you pretend to. When you wake up, you say, "I need some fresh air," and then you stride outside, Ezana thought. And he did exactly what he imagined step by step.

Outside at the most beautiful view in Aksum, he inhaled the fresh air facing while The Church of St. Mary of Zion and Stelae Park. The trip to the ancient Kingdom of Aksum changed his perspective tremendously.

He knew a lot now. He singled out the Obelisk of Ezana and concentrated on it for a moment. He learned in his miraculous journey how the Obelisk of Ezana was carved and erected. He panned his eyes to the church, which also rang many bells to him from the trip.

This is the mother of all churches in Ethiopia and Eritrea, he thought.

Ezana reflected on his experience of both worlds, and he desires to see his precious friend, the lovebird. He stepped back, sat on one of the empty chairs, and waited eagerly, praying that the bird showed up before his parents panicked and came looking for him.

Suddenly, some fluid hit him on the face. He wiped it off and looked up to the sky. The bird was chuckling above him.

"Oh, bird!" Ezana yelled.

The lovebird landed down on a table next to him. "Did you just pee on me?"

"Nope. But don't you people say it's good luck anyways?"

"Never mind. We have a lot to catch up on. Please take me out of here," Ezana begged.

"Sure. Do you want to walk or fly?"

"Fly, of course." He looked around. "But can you do the transformation right here right now?"

"Yes, you know I'm invisible," the lovebird said. "But I can't go to the past right now."

Ezana looked around nervously. "It's okay. Let's just fly in the present for a while. I want to talk."

The lovebird metamorphosed to the gigantic version of herself in a couple of minutes. Ezana hopped on, and they flew to the right toward the palace of King Kaleb, where the mysterious time machine was located.

"Bird, why did you ignore me the other day? Thanks to you, my parents think I'm a lunatic."

"What was I supposed to do?"

"You could say hello to Mom, and that would close the case."

"Sorry, but I can't be visible to everyone. Only to those I am assigned to."

The lovebird reduced the airspeed and descended for landing at the ground close to King Kaleb's palace.

When touched down, Ezana jumped off and witnessed the phenomenon of the bird shrinking back to her regular size. When she settled in her usual size and sound, Ezana pleaded, "Please help me convince my parents this," he pointed at her and himself, "happened between you and me."

"Hey, wait for a second. What did you say happened to you?"

"After my grandparents found my bed empty in the middle of the night, they called my parents and reported it to the police. Many people and the police searched for me for many hours. You can imagine how painful that could be to my family," Ezana said.

"Fast forward, as you know, miraculously, I was back in bed in the morning. And when Mom and Dad grilled me, I told them about us."

"Then?" the lovebird asked.

"They thought a demon-possessed me, and they took me to the church for exorcism."

"What do you mean, demon-possessed?" the lovebird asked seriously.

"You know, they thought I lost my mind, or I became a lunatic something."

The lovebird exploded to her peculiar laughter.

"This is not supposed to be funny, you know," Ezana said.

She rolled on the ground in hysterics. Ezana walked away and sat on the edge of the ruined castle until she finished her performance, as he liked to call it. The sweet sound and the impressive movement she made when she laughed looked and sounded like a superb show. Even though he was mad, he couldn't disregard the beauty of her laughter.

After laughing shamelessly enough, the lovebird got up and shook her feathers to dust off. She walked over and sat next to Ezana in a formal manner.

"Sorry about that," she said in a friendly tone. "So, what do you want me to do?"

"I was hoping if you could do something to convince my parents that this surreal is real. Otherwise, my life will be complicated," Ezana said gloomily.

The lovebird thought for a moment in silence. Ezana already worried not to be long, and his parents go searching for him. He looked at his watch.

"I have an idea. Follow me to the time machine," the lovebird said and paced toward the castle of King Kaleb.

"I don't have much time, you know."

"I know it won't take long. Only a few days back in history."

She went down, and he followed her to the underground of the castle where the extraordinary magic happened.

***

Tsehay woke up from a sweet nap. Yared still slept next to her. She turned onto her back, rubbed her eyes with both hands, and looked at the ceiling. Then she realized that Ezana went out before Yared and herself went to take a nap. She got out of bed and grabbed a sweater on her way out.

While Tsehay was passing through the glassed restaurant, she saw Ezana outside talking to someone who was out of her sight.

Ezana and the lovebird just landed back at the spot. Ezana thanked the bird for the unbelievable experience and her incredible help.

"Are you happy?" the lovebird asked.

"Are you kidding? I'm over the moon."

"That's the most important. Now go work on your jokes."

"You got it, bird."

Tsehay didn't expect to see Ezana talking alone again, and she couldn't believe what she was witnessing. She couldn't get closer to hug him. Her legs got weak and betrayed her. She wanted to call him, but her mouth just remained open and dry.

"Uh, oh. You are in trouble," the lovebird said, signaling Ezana to look behind him.

He turned back and saw his mom on the ground on her knees, moaning.

"Good luck, and see you tomorrow," the lovebird said and disappeared.

Ezana ran to his mom. He helped her to stand up and walk back to the hotel room. Her body was shaking, and tears were flowing down her face. Ezana felt sorry for his mother, but he didn't panic about the incident.

The lovebird showed him something that he kept as his secret weapon to prove himself to his parents. He knew when to use it, and for now, he wanted them to believe the evil spirit still possessed him.

Ezana and the lovebird discussed the only way to get time to perform his comedy gig in the past would be to extend the exorcism rite. For that reason, he should stay in the character of the evil-possessed boy.

Yared was in a deep sleep, snoring. Tsehay started crying out loud when she got in the room, which woke up Yared.

"What...what...happened? What...what's wrong?" Yared stammered, not fully awake.

Nobody answered his question. Tsehay couldn't control her emotion to talk, and Ezana preferred to give his mom the chance to tell his dad why she was crying. Yared went straight to the bathroom, soaked his face in cold water, and came back wide awake. Ezana offered his mom a glass of water and sat back confidently, waiting to explain what happened.

Yared embraced and soothed his wife like a baby until she stopped crying. Tsehay wiped her face, sipped some water, and cleaned her throat. Yared was impatient and gestured for her to start speaking.

"Baby, can we have some privacy?" Tsehay asked Ezana.

"Sure," he said and went into his room.

"He did it again," Tsehay whispered.

"Did again what?" Yared asked, hungry for more information.

"He was talking alone again."

Yared released her and walked back to a chair. He sat with head down hopelessly for a moment.

"What exactly was he talking about?" Yared asked.

"I couldn't walk close enough to hear him. I fell."

"I'm sorry about that, hun. Let's go try to figure it out over snack."

"We can't leave him alone," Tsehay said in a concerned tone.

"We are going together," Yared said. "And please be strong. Let's not show him our anxiety."

Yared walked to Ezana's room where he found him, unlike them, relaxed and focused on his world.

"We're going out. Let's go," Yared said.

Tsehay needed to wash her face, dressed up, and put on some makeup.

In that time window, in the hotel's parking lot, Yared tested Ezana by a quiz game they always played. Ezana answered without missing any. His thinking sounded clear to Yared.

Tsehay did her best to look good. Yared and Ezana noticed how she changed into elegance within a few minutes. Yared kissed her on the cheek and opened the front seat car door for her.

Yared started the engine and turned to Ezana. "What is it that scientists say makes everyone happy?"

"Ice cream!" Ezana screamed.

They all chuckled from the idea and the way Ezana answered the question. Yared cruised down from the hotel and passed through between The Church of St. Mary of Zion and the Stelae Park to the part of the city where they enjoyed several flavors of ice cream the other day.

"So, when are we leaving?" Ezana asked.

The question surprised both Tsehay and Yared, and it took them moments to respond. They communicated by just looking at each other.

"We didn't decide yet, baby," Tsehay said.

"Yes, we'll decide and let you know later," Yared added.

"Cool," Ezana said. The plan is working.

Ezana got his favorite vanilla ice cream on a cone, Tsehay got strawberry in a cup, and Yared surprised them by getting himself chocolate ice cream on a cone.

"Who doesn't like to be happy?" Yared asked.

"Awesome choice, Dad," Ezana said. "Let me give you a couple of quick, exciting ice cream facts."

"Okay, I'm listening," Yared said.

Ezana licked his ice cream good before he started dropping facts.

"The United States produces most ice cream than anywhere else in the world. And the ice cream industry moves over twenty-one billion dollars in the United States alone."

"I didn't know that," Yared said. "Honey, did you?"

"No," Tsehay said. "What else, baby?"

They wanted Ezana to continue talking, and both displayed interest.

After a series of lickings, Ezana continued. "The end of World War II was celebrated by eating ice cream."

"Wow!" Tsehay said.

"Interesting!" Yared said. "How did you know all this?"

"The amazing Internet, Dad."

"My baby is smart," Tsehay said proudly.

Deep down, Tsehay and Yared were happier not because of the facts but because of Ezana's head being on straight.

"You want to hear more?" Ezana asked. Both nodded at the same time.

"More interesting facts are coming." Ezana licked a couple of times from the melting side of his ice cream. "Vanilla is the most popular flavor of ice cream. Chocolate and strawberry follow as second and third. So, I'm enjoying the most liked ice cream, and you are working on numbers two and three."

Tsehay and Yared grinned.

"Good to know. Next time, I'll go up to number one," Tsehay said.

"I'm almost there. I'll get there before you, honey," Yared said, looking at his wife affectionately.

"Great. Wait for me over there," Tsehay teased.

They laughed again. Nobody dared to address the white elephant in the room and spoil the beautiful evening. When Ezana went to the washroom, Tsehay and Yared discussed extending the holy water bathing at the church to the seven-day rite.

***

On the fourth day at the holy water bathing, the priest was surprised to see them, and he couldn't hide it from his face. He pulled out his hand cross from his chest pocket and let the three of them kiss it. Then he reached for a jar and sprinkled holy water on their faces and spoke some words of blessings.

Yared politely asked to talk to the priest in private, updated him on Ezana's status, and informed him of the family's decision to extend the holy water bathing for the seven-day rite.

Ezana didn't know for how long their stay extended, and he wanted to make sure they stayed long enough for he to do the comedy show in the 4th century. So, he screamed when the priest poured the holy water over his head. Tsehay and Yared startled in the waiting room.

The priest smiled and started his ritual. He poured more holy water and patted Ezana on the head and the back with his hand cross and yelled some words to the evil spirit that possessed him. The priest did the same thing over and over again. Ezana screamed and shouted, imitating the people he listened before him.

"The evil spirit finally showed up!" Yared exclaimed.

62

AMERICAN OR CANADIAN?

E zana now became confident about his extended stay in Aksum for the holy water bathing. Also, he had crucial information that helped him bargain with his parents.

Relaxed, he started preparing for his comedy gig in a port city of the 4th century. He listed his favorite comedians of all time and went through their best comedy bits. But deciding which comedian's bits could be relatable and funny for the 4th-century audience became problematic. He needed his dad's help. He thought Yared's taste of comedy might be the closest to the ancient Aksumites. He wanted to do some research on him.

"Dad, who's your favorite comedian?"

Yared thought for a second. "I forgot his name...he's an old American actor."

"Steve Martin?" Ezana snapped.

"No. He has gray hair like Steve Martin though. He's in *Naked Gun, Airplane*, and *Wrongly Accused*. His movies make me laugh the most. I don't think you know him."

Ezana Googled the movies. "His name is Leslie Nielsen, and he's not an American. He's Canadian."

Yared leaned back, stunned. "All my life, I thought he was American."

Tsehay overheard their dialogue and laughed alone.

Inspired by Yared's confusion over his favorite comedian, Ezana announced later that night at dinner a game called *American or Canadian?* His parents welcomed the idea of the game. He explained how the game worked, and they were thrilled to play.

"Ladies first. Mom, Ellen DeGeneres: American or Canadian?"

"Easy. She is American."

Ezana made the sound effect for a correct answer buzzer. "Dad, Celine Dion: American or Canadian?"

"American, of course" Yared replied.

Ezana made the sound effect for a wrong answer buzzer. Yared's mouth and eyes opened wide. Tsehay laughed.

"You're up next, Mom. Jim Carrey?"

"He is one of my favorite Americans!" Tsehay exclaimed confidently.

Ezana made the sound effect for a wrong answer. Yared laughed.

"Are you sure he's not American, baby?" Tsehay asked.

"A million percent, Mom. Dad, Denzel Washington?"

"American?" Yared answered quizzically.

Ezana stayed silent for suspense. "You got it, Dad!"

Yared cheered loudly.

"Take it easy, Dad. That was super easy," Ezana said. "Mom, Mariah Carey?"

"She is American diva."

"Correcto, Mom. Dad, James Cameron?"

"American, no doubt," Yared said.

"You got it...wrong!" Ezana exclaimed. Yared wanted to argue, but Ezana quickly moved to the next one.

"Mom, Jerry Seinfeld?"

"American comedian, born and raised in New York."

Ezana nodded for correct. "Dad, Drake?"

"I don't know him," Yared answered.

"Dude! How come you don't know him?" Ezana asked.

Yared laughed.

"Mom?"

"American rapper."

"Nope. He's Canadian," Ezana said and moved to the next question without giving any window for Tsehay to argue or question.

"Dad, Keanu Reeves: American or Canadian?"

"I know him very well. He's American."

"Wrong!" Ezana moved to the next one. "Mom, Lauryn Hill?"

"Easy, she is an American hip hop superstar."

"Good job, Mom. Dad, Justin Bieber: American or Canadian?"

"I don't know him."

"Mom, same question."

"I remember you told me that he is Canadian."

"Dad, Elon Musk?"

"American."

"You sure, Dad?"

"Positive!" Yared exclaimed.

Tsehay burst into laughter. Ezana made the sound effect for a wrong answer. Yared's mouth and eyes opened wide again. Tsehay kept laughing.

"He's a citizen of South Africa, Canada, and the United States," Ezana said.

Yared argued for one-third point and quit playing.

63

THE LAST TRIP TO THE PAST

Unusually, Ezana wanted to go to bed early. Since they all would wake up early to go to church, his parents liked the idea and encouraged him to do so. He locked up his room and kept working on the jokes he found on the Internet until midnight.

He read all the "Top Ten Jokes of All Time," but most of them employed modern expressions and technologies. The Internet, cars, computers, and phones all couldn't correlate with the ancient audience.

Ezana even tried to edit some of them, but they lost their essence in the process. The bits couldn't be as funny as their original.

He put his tablet away and started thinking about the nature of the comedy show. He remembered what the lovebird told him. The mayor of the port city took anyone who bombed on stage and threw them to the mouths of his lions. A shiver ran down Ezana's spine as he realized that could happen to him.

Half-hour to midnight, Ezana got dressed in his sportswear and Nike shoes. He opened his window, threw pillows out, and jumped out as quietly as possible. The pillows saved him both from harming himself and making a sound. Within a few minutes, he met the lovebird at the usual time and place.

"I couldn't get used to it," Ezana said when he saw the lovebird morphing into her enormous version.

She waved him to hop on once she finished morphing and explained to him how the nature of birds inspired humans to invent the airplane.

"God created humans," she continued. "If you can rely on planes, technology, medical surgery, and weather predictions—all created by humans—you shouldn't be afraid to rely on things created by God."

"You're right," Ezana yelled, leaning toward her right ear.

She landed at the gate of King Kaleb's palace. Ezana hopped off and stepped back to watch her shrink to her regular size.

"Are you ready to hear my bits?" Ezana asked, stepping down the stairs.

"No. If I hear your jokes now, I won't be excited later. For spontaneous reasons, you know," the lovebird said.

Ezana intended to test his jokes and decide which bits fit the crowd, but the lovebird didn't help.

The secret door opened at 1:00 A.M, and everything happened so fast after that.

The divine gate landed Ezana and the lovebird at the seashore of the ancient port city of Adulis. Ezana remembered the lovebird took him there for an episode in the two white brothers' history. He loved the shore, but he didn't get the chance to enjoy it back then.

He closed his eyes, smelled the pleasing aroma, breathed in the fresh air, and listened to the sound of the waves the Red Sea made. There were many ships and boats nearby, but Ezana couldn't hear anything other than the sound of pure nature.

"Everybody has gone to the show. Let's go," the lovebird said as if she read his mind.

Since he attended the entertainment event of King Ella Amida, Ezana was dying to go on stage and show the ancient audience what real comedy was. He thought even the show would be the highlight of his marvelous journey to the past.

When he got closer to the stage and heard people applauding and lions roaring, he felt his heart beating fast. He wanted to ask the lovebird for her plan on how to save him from the lions if his jokes failed to make the audience laugh, but he wanted to show confidence in his materials.

Is it even possible to die in the past? He created a dialogue balloon with a question mark in his head.

People like Amelia Earhart have mysteriously vanished from planet earth, a reply came on another dialogue balloon.

"You sound worried. Are you?" the lovebird asked.

Ezana almost said, "Very." but he took it back.

"I'm good. I am just working on my bits. Rehearsing, you know," Ezana said.

"That's great. I can't wait to see you on stage." She beamed. "By the way, do you have a stage name? You can't go on stage as Ezana, you know."

Ezana nodded. "I know it's the king's name. Let me think about it."

The name change didn't cross Ezana's mind. But many things were happening opposite to his expectations that day. It never occurred to him the event would be that big and famous. He thought it would be a house party the mayor and his friends enjoyed. He was wrong. The show was so grand that residents and workers of the port city flooded to the venue. The audience looked to enjoy the show tremendously.

"I didn't know people were crazy about the show," Ezana said.

"Some of the audiences enjoy the entertaining shows. Some of them enjoy the agony of the performers thrown to the lions," the lovebird said.

Ezana startled when the bird mentioned the lions. The more Ezana got closer to the venue, the roar of the audience became more prominent and louder.

The lovebird told Ezana to stop and explained to him the rules of the game and how she would include his name into the list of the performers. Ezana felt another hit of adrenaline when the bird finished the explanation without mentioning anything about the exit strategy if his bits failed to be funny.

Maybe she's confident about my bits, Ezana thought.

64

THE LIFE OR DEATH SHOW

The mayor of the port city, who was a close friend of the late king, Ella Amida, built one of the best amphitheaters in the kingdom. A wired fence separated the audience and the stage. There were two dark holes with direct access to the performing stage area, but no one noticed them until the show started and a performer's act failed. The mayor decided who was funny or not after a glance at his wife. No matter how any performer entertained the audience or made them laugh, if the mayor's wife didn't feel entertained or didn't smile, he would end up in the lions' belly.

The exotic and exciting show attracted the audience. The expensive jewelry rewards attracted domestic and foreign performers. Ezana, carrying the lovebird on his shoulder, arrived at the gates of the amphitheater. The vibe around the venue reminded him of modern-day events like the NBA and the NFL. People excited to get inside the small version of the Colosseum made long lines. Tickets, food, and drinks were selling like hotcakes at all gates.

Ezana and the lovebird sat invisible two rows behind the mayor's seat. The arena was packed and ready. The lovebird asked Ezana for his stage name. He went through the list of names he had in his mind and gave her one. She smiled and flew behind the stage of the amphitheater.

"Attending this incredible event would be more than enough," Ezana spoke to himself. He was super happy as an audience member but extremely anxious as a featured performer.

The lovebird came back. "You are performer number eight!"

"Thanks a lot, bird," Ezana said in a shaking voice.

The announcer asked the audience to stand up and welcome their esteemed mayor and his beloved wife. The audience stood and greeted the mayor warmly. After the mayor and his entourage took their seats, the announcer presented the lineup of the acts. Magicians, comedians, and singers from both local and abroad lined up for one of the greatest shows in the Aksumite Kingdom.

A local singer with a flute opened the show. The audience sang with him.

"He must be a famous musician," Ezana said.

The lovebird nodded. "I think so. Even the mayor's wife didn't take her eyes off him."

People gave him a standing ovation. The mayor signaled to the master of the ceremony, and the singer was allowed to sit on the winners' bench.

A magician took the stage next. He did fire magic and moved everyone to the edge of their seats. On the final trick, a small dog caught on fire, cried in agony, and changed the happy vibe to sadness.

Someone came with a vessel of water and splashed it on the dog. The dog was saved.

A huge bodyguard came out from the back and threw the magician off the stage to the lions' space. The dark holes opened, and the lions came roaring. Most of the people, including Ezana, turned their faces away. The man screamed and fought for his life, but that didn't last long.

The announcer yelled two names. An Arab couple took the stage, and the sound of agony was replaced by the sound of Arab music. The couple greeted the audience humbly. The man sat on the corner of the stage and started playing his musical instrument, the Qanun. The woman waited for her moment and exploded into a sensual belly dance. The audience cheered. The atmosphere completely changed as if a lion didn't eat a man alive a few minutes ago.

Ezana was faking a smile to the lovebird. He was scared and wanted to run away to the future, but he felt like he represented the 21st century and didn't want to let down the billions of people whom he was representing. He thought it was like the Olympics between the past and the present.

"The past shouldn't defeat the present," Ezana said unconsciously.

"That's a great spirit. Let's go backstage and get ready. It's almost time," the lovebird said.

Still invisible, Ezana and the lovebird entered backstage. People of all colors, sexes, shapes, and sizes were all over the room, silent. They were rehearsing, praying, and meditating. The silence in the room gave Ezana pain in his stomach. The lovebird motivated him as if he was going to a boxing fight.

"Once you are in the backstage, there is no way out. Everyone must go there, perform, and accept the verdict of the mayor," the lovebird explained. "That's why they call it The Life or Death Show."

That was the fact, but it didn't motivate Ezana.

The audience cheered after a Greek comedian's funny jokes. That meant staying alive and getting expensive jewelry. The performers backstage smiled with hope, and all looked at the next in line. The little man from Roma put his snake and pigeons in a bag and carried a monkey on his shoulder. All wished him good luck.

The announcer called his name. The man from Roma crossed himself and marched to the stage. The audience cheered for him and continued cheering for his incredible talent. But everyone knew that the cheering from the fans didn't matter if the mayor's wife didn't like him.

It was too late even to be worried. Ezana tried to focus on his jokes.

"What language am I using?" Ezana asked.

"You are empowered to speak all three languages: Ge'ez, Sabean, and Greek," the lovebird said.

"Sweet. I'll go with Ge'ez."

"When you are ready, just sip water from that barrel," the lovebird said. "Then you know you will be visible." Ezana nodded. "I'm ready."

He walked to the barrel and sipped some water. Suddenly, he was among the performers, and all jolted except a magician who saved Ezana.

"Magnificent magic," the magician said.

Then all thought that was super magic and relaxed. The magicians marveled at the trick they never experienced before. Some of them panicked that if he performed before them, they would be dinner of the lions. The fear and excitement of his fellow performers gave Ezana hope.

A beautiful smiling woman dressed in a lovely silk costume came out on stage accompanied by a musician with a flute. The spectators loved her at first sight. She waved to the audience, walking from corner to corner of the stage. When she was ready, and the audience's cheer fell to silence, the musician started blowing the flute. The woman tried to sing but couldn't. She gave it a try again, but nothing came out.

Something went wrong. The audience cheered to encourage her. It looked she lost her voice on the stage.

The musician, who was her husband, panicked. He reached out to her, put his hand around her, whispered something to her ear, and kissed her. He walked back to his position and started playing again.

Then he stopped and waited for her to start singing. She opened her mouth and gave it another try, but it didn't work.

Instead, tears flowed down on her cheeks. Some people in the audience started booing her. The husband threw his flute on the ground, ran, and hugged her tight. They both begged the audience for mercy.

The bodyguard marched toward them and knocked them both down off the stage into the lions' territory. The woman screamed, the man shouted for forgiveness, and the audience howled. The lions were unleashed from the cages. The next scene was painful for the couple and a joyful dinner for the big cats.

The audience sounded angry by the verdict over the couple, especially the beautiful woman with the lovely silk dress. Some even wept for her. Performers who won the hearts of the mayor and his wife were destined to watch the tragic fates of their fellow performers from the winners' bench chair.

After the lions got back to their cages, janitors replaced them and cleaned their dining table. Then the announcer called out the next act.

65

THE BOY FROM THE FUTURE

T he boy from the future," the announcer yelled. The name
caught everyone's attention, including the mayor, his wife, and
his entourage.

"The boy from the future, come out!" the announcer yelled again.
Ezana stepped up the stairs from the backstage room and appeared in
the center of the stage. The audience leaned back in awe. His clothes,
shoes, and even his hair cut were strange to the audience. It was dead
silence. Ezana tried to walk and talk to prove himself that he wasn't an
alien, but he stumbled and stood clueless.

"Nice costume, boy!" a person in the audience shouted.

And those three magic words changed everything—the audience's
judgment adjusted. They accepted Ezana as an artist with a unique
costume.

Ezana thanked the man who shouted and presented his first joke.
Nobody laughed. No one understood the joke. The audience was so
quiet that Ezana could hear the roaring of the lions down from the
dungeon. Ezana shared another bit, which he remixed to adapt the
terms and technological to the 4th-century audience. This time the
audience started to moan and whine.

The mayor became impatient and kept checking his wife's face for a
signal. The mayor's wife stared at Ezana, hoping he would say something

funny before she sent the signal. The air in the entire amphitheater got intense. Ezana stood on stage, confused, and panicked.

Suddenly, a peal of laughter emerged. All looked around to see who was making that beautiful sound of laughter. Only Ezana could see the invisible lovebird, and her laughter relieved him from his anxiety.

The exceptional laughter of the bird distracted the verdict over Ezana. The audience didn't understand who was laughing and why but enjoyed it for a moment.

But the mayor didn't like it. He didn't favor anything that was beyond his control. The invisible laughter bothered him.

"Okay, that's enough," the mayor said.

Ezana knew the lovebird couldn't control her involuntary laugh, and his anxiety came back again. He didn't want the mayor to be angry or nervous while he was still on the stage. The mysterious laughter of the lovebird continued.

"Stop laughing!" the mayor exploded. He pointed his finger at Ezana. "Boy, do you have anything to do with this?"

Ezana didn't know what to say. He wanted to run back, but there was no way out. Winners went to the bench. Losers went to the lions— no other option. No exit. The thing among the mysterious laughter, the angry mayor, and the clueless boy became an exciting puzzle for the audience. Everyone moved to the edge of their seats when the mayor started walking furiously to the stage. And the bodyguard who knocked the losers off the stage moved toward Ezana from behind. Ezana saw both men approaching him from different directions.

"Bird!" he shouted in desperation.

Then a couple of seconds later, he vanished. Again, the audience leaned back, astonished by the sudden disappearance of the boy from the future. Most of the people put their hands on their mouths. The mayor and the bodyguard froze in the middle and looked around and up in the air. It seemed the most suspenseful show of the kingdom.

While Ezana was invisible, the lovebird suggested aborting the show and going back to the future. However, Ezana insisted on finishing what he has started. Then to the audience's surprise, Ezana reappeared on the stage.

"He's back!" people shouted, extremely excited.

Ezana never left the stage. The lovebird just touched him to go invisible for his safety.

"Great magic trick!" a magician on the winners' bench yelled and gave Ezana a standing ovation.

All the winners followed the magician to applaud the boy from the future. The entire audience stood up and cheered for Ezana. The mayor, who stood still, waved to the bodyguard and walked back to his seat. The bodyguard got the message and retreated to the corner of the stage. Everybody thought that was his last show and expected him to sit on the winners' bench.

Ezana, the boy from the future with extreme magic tricks, beamed.

Exhilarated, glanced at the lovebird. She gave him two wings up with a huge smile, which encouraged him to milk the moment of his accidental fame.

The spectators sat on the edge of their seats, their mouths and eyes wide opened to capture what the boy from the future would do next.

They stared at Ezana without blinking so that they didn't miss his unusual magic trick. But contrary to their expectation, Ezana told a joke he got from the Internet, which he thought they would understand:

"Sherlock Holmes and Dr. Watson decide to go on a camping trip.

After dinner and a bottle of wine, they laid down for the night and went to sleep.

"Some hours later, Holmes awoke and nudged his faithful friend.

'Watson, look up at the sky and tell me what you see.'

"Watson replied, 'I see millions of stars.'

"'What does that tell you?'

"Watson pondered for a minute. 'Astronomically, it tells me that there are millions of galaxies and potentially billions of planets. Astrologically, I observe that Saturn is in Leo. Horologically, I deduce that the time is approximately a quarter past three. Theologically, I can see that God is all-powerful and that we are small and insignificant. Meteorologically, I suspect that we will have a beautiful day tomorrow.

What does it tell you, Holmes?'

"Holmes was silent for a minute and then spoke, 'Watson, you idiot. Someone has stolen our tent!'"

Ezana finished telling the joke, laughed, and waited for a huge laugh. The lovebird quickly understood the audience didn't get the bit and moved to save the moment. She landed on Ezana's shoulder, and the audience's minds exploded in amazement again. He vanished into thin air.

"He did it again!" the magician shouted.

Most of the people rocketed from their seats and looked up and around in the sky. Many yelled to express their astonishment. Ezana and the lovebird, still on the stage, listened to the appreciation and exhilaration of the audience. Ezana sipped water and appeared again. People went crazy. The whole audience, including the mayor and his wife, gave him a standing ovation. On the lovebird's advice, Ezana bowed to the audience and walked to the winners' bench.

After such a phenomenal show, the mayor came out on the stage and announced the end of the excellent show. He explained how his wife and himself were thrilled by the boy's magical performance that they had never seen before. Then he called his wife to the stage to present prizes to the winners. The Boy from the Future took the grand prize. Ezana received a bag of jewelry and a kiss from the mayor's wife.

Right after the kiss, the lovebird hopped on his shoulder, and he disappeared while all eyes were on him. The audience clapped and shouted. Then everyone waited to see what the boy would do next. But nothing happened. Ezana and the lovebird left.

66

INVISIBLE SANTA

Outside the amphitheater, Ezana and the lovebird opened the prize bag, and their faces glowed by the reflection of the gold and other gems projected on their faces. Ezana jumped in a thrill and was awed by the quality and quantity of the gifts.

"I have bad news for you," the lovebird said.

Ezana closed the bag and looked at the bird with a blank face.

"I'm sorry. You can't take anything from the past," the lovebird added.

Ezana froze for a while. "Okay, I have an idea, and I always dreamed of doing it," Ezana said and started walking.

A couple of hours later, several beggars became rich quickly.

Precious stones sprinkled from nowhere in the streets of Adulis and Aksum. People in both cities flooded to the streets after the news of the gemstones spread. The invisible Ezana enjoyed listening and watching the reactions of the lucky people who became rich in a matter of seconds.

He asked the lovebird to fly him around in the kingdom before they left for the future. Then he did more random kindness by throwing the rest of the gemstones from the sky down on farmers working in fields, on women washing clothes in rivers, on people going to the market, and on young shepherds.

Most of the people were humble and grateful. Ezana and the lovebird heard them saying, "Thank you, Lord." There were also some greedy who looked and asked for more.

"Feels good?" the lovebird asked after they finished the giveaway and landed on the ground in the Aksumite Kingdom.

"It feels wonderful. Every time we came here was a thrill. It's super awesome!" Ezana said. "This is beyond a dream come true. I used to dream of being invisible. I became invisible, plus Santa."

"I'm glad to hear that," the lovebird said, shrinking down to her regular size.

"Thank you so much for everything," Ezana said, pressing his hands together and bowing as Indians do.

"Thank God, not me," the lovebird replied, looking up in the sky.

Ezana, still pressing his hands together, looked up to the air too and thanked God.

"And speaking of God," the lovebird said, "The Life or Death Show was canceled by King Ezana after the kingdom officially became a Christian state. I just took you a little back in time before Ezana became king."

"Right decision. Throwing people to the lions alive was brutal."

The lovebird led Ezana to the nearest divine gate, and they were back in the future and never returned to the past.

67

THE KISS THAT SAVED EZANA

In the present day of Aksum city, Tsehay and Yared woke up by the alarm at 5:00 A.M. Tsehay knocked on Ezana's room. "Get up, baby. Time to go to the church."

Yared and Tsehay got ready, but Ezana's room remained closed.

Tsehay knocked, calling his name repeatedly. Yared couldn't stand it and pushed the door open. They couldn't believe what they saw: an empty bed and an opened window.

Tsehay ran to the window and saw the pillows outside on the ground. She felt her legs getting weaker and weaker to the point she couldn't trust them to carry her body. She turned around, pushed her back against the wall and slid down to the floor. As soon as she hit the floor, her tears rolled down her cheeks. Yared hopelessly joined her on the floor. They sat side by side in silence until a knock on the door woke them up from their profound thoughts.

Yared jumped up and walked to open the hotel door. Ezana was behind the door wearing his best smile.

"Hun, he's here!" Yared shouted.

Suddenly, Tsehay's weak legs became energetic, and she leaped up and ran to the door. Ezana's parents were so happy to see him that their waves of anger swept away.

Many hugs and kisses later, Ezana asked them if they wanted to take him for the holy water baptism or want his explanation about his adventurous trip. Tsehay and Yared preferred to go to the church. His parents were more suspicious than ever about their son's well-being.

They sat behind the curtain of the holy water rite room. Ezana didn't scream or anything unusual during the entire ritual. The fifth day ceremony went normal.

At breakfast, Ezana told them a leftover joke from his performance in the past. It happened to be an excellent treat for his parents after such a stressful morning. They laughed both at the hilarity of the joke and that their son sounded sane.

Ezana liked the pleasant feeling he created, and he sensed the urge to address the elephant in the room.

"Mom, Dad, can I have your attention for a couple of minutes?" Ezana asked, using a tissue to clean up himself.

His parents became attentive and ready to listen to him.

"Sure, baby," Tsehay said.

"Take all the time you want, son."

"Thanks," Ezana said and took some time to compose his speech.

Although Tsehay and Yared were so eager to hear what he was going to tell them, they waited until he began speaking.

"I know you have been worried since the incident of that night. You think something terrible happened to me, and I don't blame you for that. What happened is unimaginable. But if you give me a chance to explain, I can convince you that what I told you about the bird is accurate," Ezana said.

Tsehay and Yared, though they seemed anxious to go there, looked at each other and let him explain. Ezana glowed and started telling the story from the beginning. He told how and when the lovebird approached him and the power she commanded to be invisible and transform herself into a gigantic beast. His level of excitement and some of the historical keywords he dropped in the middle gained him their attention, but they didn't buy it at all.

"It sounds like you had a series of beautiful dreams, son. And I'm glad you have read some of my books in the room. Your knowledge of history has tremendously improved," Yared said. "What do you think, honey?" Yared asked Tsehay.

"Some of it sounds real and some a dream," Tsehay said carefully so as not to hurt Ezana's feelings.

His parents wished they could believe what he said, but they didn't, and the kind of honesty and integrity they set as a rule in the family didn't allow them to pretend. They dared to react sincerely and accept the consequences, but they couldn't see any sign of anger on Ezana. He didn't lose his cool. He asked their permission again to add some more pieces of evidence to his explanation. His parents agreed to hear and waited with great enthusiasm. Ezana knew he had one last chance to convince them, and he didn't want to blow it.

"I have to go to the restroom real quick. Excuse me," Ezana said.

He wanted time to craft his secret weapon story that he selected with the help of the lovebird at the time machine.

"Oh, my baby. It's killing me to see him working hard to convince us," Tsehay said, putting her right hand on her chest, unconsciously expressing her heartfelt love.

"I was so thrilled my beautiful wife is back, but now, this is breaking my heart into pieces," Yared said, and suddenly broke into tears.

Tsehay didn't expect that and stopped dead for a moment. Then she realized it wouldn't be an inspiring scene for Ezana. She pulled out a napkin from her purse, wiped his tears from his face, and whispered to him to stop before she started crying too.

The round trip to the bathroom gave Ezana the chance to prepare. His parents received him with some extra fake smiles on their faces, and he sensed the atmosphere was not the same as he left it.

"We are dying to hear what you have to say, baby," Tsehay said.

Yared nodded to strengthen the idea.

"Okay, okay, but promise me to stay open-minded and listen without interrupting," Ezana said and sat comfortably to tell the story.

They both agreed to his preconditions. Ezana connected his mind with the images he saw during his magical journey with the lovebird back to his parents' short trip to Kafta Sheraro National Park.

"I'm positive this will end the argument," Ezana said and explained to his parents how a great time they had at the Kafta Sheraro National Park. Tsehay and Yared nodded their heads in encouragement while listening.

Ezana added details like what kinds of animals and birds they saw and how the park was beyond their expectations. Especially how they reacted when they encountered a lion. They listened attentively. He added more details of their visit to Dedebit, the patriot Sihul's family house in Shire Endasilassie and General Hayelom Araya's memorial statue at his birthplace of Addi Nebrid.

"So, what do you say now?" Ezana asked eagerly.

Tsehay turned her face to her husband.

Yared fidgeted his fingers and carefully said, "All you have said is true, but..."

"But what, Dad?"

"We told all the things you said to my parents the other day when you were asleep in the next room." Yared turned to his wife, hoping she would agree with what he said.

"You know what, baby? You overheard us telling our experience to your grandma and grandpa while you were sleeping. And maybe the stories we told them were interwoven in your dreams," Tsehay said.

"What about the kiss you shared?" Ezana fired back. He unleashed his secret weapon.

Tsehay's face flushed scarlet. Yared looked at his wife and froze for a moment. Ezana faced down, and awkward silence took place.

"What kiss?" Yared shouted without thinking.

Ezana tilted his head up, and he let the words slip out of his mouth.

"In the Kafta Sheraro Park, you asked the guide to get you water from the car, and you kissed when he strode away."

Tsehay and Yared were shocked. They looked at each other, and both gazed at Ezana with complete amazement. He knew he pushed the correct button.

"Do you want me to explain your kiss scene under the beautiful tree?" Ezana asked.

Tsehay and Yared never share their private business with anyone. The fact that he mentioned that particular information changed everything.

"No. It's not necessary, baby," Tsehay whispered sheepishly.

"Dad?" Ezana asked.

"I agree with your mom. You don't need to go there," Yared said.

"So, are we cool now?"

"I think we are," Tsehay said, "I'd like to hear more about your friend."

Ezana's face beamed in delight.

"I'm speechless. Congratulations. You won. But I need time to process it," Yared said.

"How about we continue the conversation later at dinner?" Tsehay asked.

Yared and Ezana nodded.

***

Yared and Tsehay felt a weight lifted off their shoulders, and they started planning the rest of their trip with bright minds. Ezana, now a free boy, went out looking for the lovebird without any tension. While he was rushing outside through the glass restaurant, he saw a bird flying away. It was a quick flash, and he couldn't be sure if that was his friend or a different bird. He sat there loaded with bliss, facing the stunning view and reflecting on the productive conversation he had with his parents.

Later at dinner, Tsehay and Yared came organized with a million questions about the bird and what happened during their multiple trips to the past. Except for one particular thing, Ezana answered and explained everything gracefully. Tsehay was crying now and then while Ezana was breaking down the story.

"Regret is killing me for not believing and giving you the chance to explain," Tsehay said.

Yared reached out and hugged her. "You are right, hun."

They apologized and asked Ezana to forgive them for their ignorance.

"I don't blame you. How could you buy such a story?" Ezana said.

"It sounds like a fantasy story from one of my comic books."

Ezana worked to destroy their regrets and bad feelings. They felt that he cleared their clouded minds and appreciated his courage to put up with them during the past few days.

"So," Yared said, "when are we going to meet the bird. You didn't address that question?"

Tsehay shook her head and added, "Yes, baby, we can't wait to meet your mysterious friend."

Ezana was deliberately avoiding that part.

"Umm...I'm afraid I don't have good news on that one," Ezana said.

Yared leaned forward, and Tsehay did the same unconsciously.

"Why? What happened to your friend?" Yared asked, concerned.

"Nothing happened," Ezana said. "When you didn't believe me, I asked the lovebird to meet you guys, but she said she was not allowed to be visible for you. I'm sorry."

When Ezana said that, Tsehay realized that was the reason she thought Ezana was talking alone like obsessed.

68

MIRACLE TREE

Tsehay and Yared finally believed the miracle phenomenon happened to their beloved son. The anxiety left their lives and was replaced with humility and joy. After Ezana went to bed, his parents stayed in the restaurant for a refreshing conversation over wine.

Around 3:00 A.M. that night, Yared woke up from a dream gasping for air. His strange move woke up Tsehay. She rubbed her eyes to see what was happening. He was sweating and wheezing. She got up, gave him a glass of water and waited until he cooled down. Yared sipped the water and took a moment to analyze the dream that woke him.

"Oh, my God!" he yelled. He leaned back to the bed's headboard and closed his eyes.

"What? What is it, hun?" Tsehay asked, taking the glass from his hand.

"I saw a dream about the car crash we had," he said, still his eyes closed.

"Sorry about that, hun. Let's go back to sleep." Tsehay tucked in.

"I think there was a miracle we didn't acknowledge." Yared became fully awake and alive.

"It was a miracle we came out of that accident unharmed, and I remembered we appreciated that," Tsehay said, followed by a yawn.

"I know, but in the dream, I saw us speeding up to crash off a cliff, and all of a sudden, the tree popped up from nowhere and saved us from falling over the cliff."

Tsehay nodded half-sleep.

"But that's not all. Do you remember what the guy who helped us was saying?" Yared asked.

"I'm very sleepy, hun. Can we talk about this later?" Tsehay murmured.

"The guy was saying, 'It's a miracle. It's a miracle.' He must have seen the miracle tree," he said excitedly. He expected her to say something. When she didn't, he checked her. She was gone, but he couldn't go back to sleep. He kept replaying the car crash scene in his head. Something hit him, and he almost jumped.

"Ezana noticed," he said to himself.

Yared got out of his bed and walked to Ezana's room. It was 3:15 A.M., and his son was in a deep sleep. He wished to wake him up and ask him, but the way Ezana slept made him change his mind. He went back to his bed, stayed awake until the first light, and went out for coffee.

69

GOODBYE, LOVEBIRD

Ezana spent a sleepless night in Aksum. He usually never had a sleeping problem. The reason for his insomnia was apparent to him. He worried about leaving Aksum without saying goodbye to the lovebird. He had many visualized balloon dialogues, questions, and answers sessions with the bird. He fell asleep around 2:00 A.M. and woke up again too early.

Out of all the imaginary conversations, questions, and answers he had, the only thing that woke up with him was, *Why was I chosen to enjoy this incredible, magical experience?*

The question urged him to meet the bird before he left the city. He grabbed his last bar of chocolate, informed his mom quickly, and rushed outside. A lovely sunrise was shining at his favorite place, the most beautiful view in Aksum. He took a chair from an empty table and put it at the edge where he could spot the lovebird coming.

Politely, he called one of the waitresses nearby and ordered scrambled eggs and orange juice for breakfast. Then he sat facing the sunrise, hoping to see his best friend for the last time. The waitress came back with a table, put it in front of him and disappeared back into the kitchen.

Ezana's breakfast came before the bird. He turned around, gave his back to the sun, and started eating.

"So, you are eating my auntie's eggs?" the lovebird asked, landing on his table.

Ezana's heart almost stopped beating. He dropped the fork and bread from his hands. "Oh, dear bird!" he exclaimed, extremely thrilled to see her. He felt his heart pounding in his throat.

She noticed the panic and said, "Relax, boy from the future!" She giggled.

He pushed the half-eaten breakfast, sipped his orange juice, and tried to be cool.

"Are you okay now?" the lovebird asked.

"Yeah," Ezana said.

"What was that all about anyway? You looked like the first day we met."

"I was afraid you wouldn't show up," Ezana said. "We are leaving tomorrow, and I didn't want to leave without saying goodbye and thanking you," Ezana said, radiating joy.

The lovebird made a sad face for a moment and broke into giggling.

"Oh, by the way, here is a treat for you," Ezana said and tossed some chocolate bars on the table.

The lovebird fainted on the table jokingly. "You have no idea how enormously I enjoy this when it melts in my mouth."

"Oh, dear bird! You should have worked in Mr. Willy Wonka's Chocolate Factory. You would enjoy the fancy chocolates!" Ezana said.

"It sounds delicious. Where is this factory?"

"Ah, my bad, it's a fictitious factory in a book called *Charlie and the Chocolate Factory*. Sorry," Ezana said. "We are leaving tomorrow, and I have lots of questions to ask you."

"Shoot one for the road."

"Why me, bird? Why am I favored to enjoy this incredible ride?" Ezana asked.

"There must be a reason or a call to adventure. Maybe you didn't pay attention, I think," the lovebird said.

"A call to adventure? My mom uses that phrase all the time."

"Cool. How about we go for your last ride and talk while flying in the air?"

"Sweet!" Ezana signed the bill of his breakfast and gave it to the waitress until the bird transformed into her gigantic size.

The lovebird was both thrilled and eager to be high in the sky and break the fabulous news to Ezana.

70

BLURRED LINE BETWEEN
REALITY AND ILLUSION

Yared and Tsehay dressed up, ready to go down for their last day in the city. They walked from their hotel room to the most beautiful view in Aksum through the restaurant, discussing how to spend their final day. When they stepped outside, they looked around, but Ezana wasn't there. There were only a couple of tourists who just arrived at the hotel and were appreciating the view.

Yared and Ezana shared the same thought without saying a word: Ezana might have met the bird.

They pulled chairs under the veranda of the glass restaurant, facing the opened air spot where Ezana and the lovebird meet. Tsehay scanned the menu and ordered breakfast for both of them.

"Did you see our son this morning?" Tsehay asked the waitress.

"Yes. I served him breakfast right there," the waitress said, politely pointing to where Ezana had breakfast.

"And did you see him leaving?" Yared asked curiously.

The waitress went through her mental notes for a moment, trying to remember. "Ah, no, sir," the waitress said.

"Thank you, dear," Tsehay said and gave her the menu back.

"So, do you think Ezana flew the bird?" Tsehay asked Yared.

"After my dream, I've started to believe everything," Yared said.

"What's happening is amazing. We are incredibly blessed."

The waitress came back with their breakfasts. "Here is oatmeal, orange juice, and green tea for you, ma'am. And here is your French toast, mixed juice, and black coffee, sir," the waitress said.

Everything was perfect as ordered. Most of the time, some waiters missed or mismatched things, but not this one.

"Bon appetit," said the waitress before she left, and Yared and Tsehay thanked her dearly.

While eating, they got lost in contemplating Ezana's life. They both believed they were not mindful enough to notice his activities, and they bounced back from their reversed memory. Instead, they preferred anticipating Ezana's reappearance from his mysterious adventure.

Yared swished the coffee in his cup absentmindedly. The waitress observed the couple's uncomfortable silence and approached them, smiling. She refilled Yared's coffee and asked them if there was anything they needed.

"We are good, and you are one of the best waitresses in town," Tsehay said, flashing a smile.

"I agree," Yared nodded.

"Thank you both. I appreciate it," the waitress said.

"You welcome. Would you bring us the bill please?" Tsehay asked.

"Sure," the waitress disappeared through the restaurant.

When they put back their table serviettes on the table and looked up, they saw Ezana walking toward them out of nowhere. They were shocked. Their eyes were away for a second, and he just appeared there. Ezana walked toward them, smiling like the astronauts when they return from a successful mission in space.

Once they recovered from the shock, they remembered that they should smile and be happy to see him.

"Did you just land from the sky?" Yared asked, trying to hide his shock.

"As a matter of fact, yes, I did," Ezana said. He wished he could break the terrific news the lovebird informed him right there.

"Look whose dream of the comic books came true!" Tsehay exclaimed. She wanted to stand up and hug him but couldn't be sure about her shaky legs.

Both Tsehay and Yared felt something strange. They realized that to think about a miracle and to see it happening were extremely different. Witnessing it gave them some chills. Ezana, on the other hand, beaming in sociable delight, pulled up a chair and joined them at the table.

For his parents, it was a blur between reality and illusion. Yared sent his fingers under his jacket and pinched himself to make sure he wasn't dreaming. Suddenly, he rocketed up from his chair and stood aimlessly. He realized that he startled Ezana and sat back quickly.

Tsehay understood what happened. She sent her hand under the table and touched him on the knee.

"Dad, are you okay?" Ezana asked, concerned.

"Perfectly okay," Yared said.

Tsehay pulled the bill and signed it to their room expenses. She calculated the amount in her head, reached into her purse, and put a generous 20 percent tip for the wonderful waitress on the table.

Ezana turned around to the most beautiful view in Aksum for the last time and walked out before them in a happy, rhythmic motion.

"Let's go say, 'Adieu,' to the monks," Yared said and hopped into his car.

They had their last soul food lunch with the monks and before going back to the hotel for final packing.

"Let's go!" Yared yelled while Tsehay and Ezana were getting their last blessings from the monks.

"Grandma, grandpa, I'll see you this time next year!" Ezana shouted, beaming in delight.

Both grandparents stood up and pressed millions of kisses on him.

"God willing, we'll be waiting for you," his grandma said pleasantly.

"And here is a little present from your grandma and me. You can hang it in your room to remember us," his grandpa handed him a wrapped gift.

71

GOING BACK TO THE MIRACLE TREE

The original itinerary was to drive back to Mekelle via a different route: the Adwa to Abiy Addi to Mekelle. But after Yared's strange dream about the miracle tree, they wanted to go back via the same road to check if what Yared dreamed was a reality.

After such an extraordinary, miraculous journey, Ezana didn't doubt the miracle tree. He didn't see the miracle tree popping up from nowhere to save them as his dad saw it in his dream. However, he knew some kind of a miracle had happened from the way the guy acted. Plus, the good guy was keeping saying, "It's a miracle."

Before leaving Aksum, Yared played back the dream in his head a million times. Their car speeding up to crash off a cliff, and they all screamed and shouted. Then all of a sudden, the tree popped up from nowhere and saved them from falling over the cliff. When they finally headed to the car accident site, which was thirty miles away, Yared steered the wheel in complete silence. Ezana was doing the same with his incredible experience with the lovebird. Tsehay, who loved to stay present all the time, guessed what was going on with her sweethearts, and she let them wander in their heads.

Yared's heart started pounding hard when they arrived near the accident scene. He pulled the car away from the location, under a shelter of trees. Tsehay checked left and right but couldn't see the site they crashed.

"It's beyond the trees. Let's walk," Yared said.

They walked to the crash site from the opposite side. Yared's heartbeat increased, but his legs were walking in slow motion. Ezana and Tsehay walked ahead of him. When they walked out of the trees and got closer to the point where they could see the crashing site, Tsehay held Ezana's hand, and they both stopped, waiting for Yared. He took Tsehay's free hand, and with her in the middle, they all held hands and strode the last few yards together. When they could see the site clearly, what they saw blew their minds.

"Oh my God!" Yared said and sank to his knees.

Tsehay did the same, and her tears rolled down her face.

Ezana ran to the site and followed the trails of their car tires. The tree that saved their lives was gone. It just popped up to protect them from falling over the cliff. Only a hole in the ground left a witness of the miracle.

They sat there for hours, counting their blessings and talking about the miracle tree, Ezana's adventure with the lovebird, and other miracles that happened in their lives.

72

BREAKING THE SECRET NEWS

In the middle of counting their blessings, Ezana struggled to hold his excellent secret news the lovebird told him. She wanted him to announce the super awesome information to his parents when they got back in the US. Still, Ezana thought the moment was perfect to break the news.

"Mom, Dad, I have more great news for us," Ezana said.

"I don't expect anything more significant than what has already happened, but shoot," Yared said.

"My friend, the lovebird, visited our future," Ezana stopped to measure their interest. He sensed both were all ears.

"And...?" Tsehay asked, enunciating the word.

"She said I'm gonna have a sister."

Ezana noticed his parents face glowing more. Tsehay stood up and knelt with her hands up in the air. She started praising God, and Yared joined her with similar emotions. Both melted into tears of joy. Ezana was moved by their reaction and paused the story for a moment. Then he decided to continue the story to save them from an emotional rollercoaster.

"The bird said the name of my sister would be Saba. She said the reason would be to honor Queen Saba for her significant role in keeping safe the Ark of Covenant," Ezana said.

His parents' jaws dropped open. They wanted to name their daughter Saba, and the precision of the detail blew their minds. Tsehay's eyes opened again, and tears rolled down her face.

"Oh, God! That was the name we had for years. My mind is about to explode," Tsehay said.

"Your mom loved the name Saba, and we would call her that if we had a daughter," Yared added.

"Perfect. God answered your prayers precisely," Ezana said, sparkling.

"Give me ten minutes. I need to do a praise meditation," Tsehay said and sat in a meditating position.

Yared felt he was in a dream. He did what he usually did when he found himself in such a state of mind. He pinched himself on the thigh secretly. When he realized it all was real, he didn't talk but smiled from ear to ear.

When Tsehay finished the praise meditation, Ezana remembered something and rocketed up from the green grass he was sitting on.

"What? What? What?" Tsehay bounced from the ground grass and jumped around like a kangaroo funnily.

Yared stood too and started looking for ants on the grass. Ezana enjoyed the show for a moment and then told them to calm down.

"I thought ants stung you, baby," Tsehay said, sitting back on the ground.

"I just remembered something the lovebird told me. How could I forget it all this time?" Ezana said. "Matthew 19:26. I want to Google it right now. Let me get my phone. Dad, the car key, please?"

Instead of the car key, Yared handed him his iPhone.

"Thanks, Dad." Ezana typed Matthew 19:26 in the search box on Google and clicked the button to search.

Tsehay and Yared looked up at him eagerly.

"Here it is," Ezana said. "Are you ready?"

"Yes, we are ready, baby," Tsehay responded passionately.

"Jesus looked at them and said, 'With man, this is impossible, but with God all things are possible.'" Ezana read the verse from the Bible, accentuating every word.

"Amen," Tsehay said more passionately than ever.

"It's true," Yared added with similar intensity.

Tsehay remembered something and whispered it to Yared's ear. Instantly his face beamed. Ezana demanded to know what made his father's face light up. Yared smiled and described how they used his twelfth birthday to celebrate their fifteenth love anniversary.

Suddenly, everything sounded right to Ezana, and he quickly jumped to questions. He asked them why they acted so weird at Yeha and Abba Garima Monastery. Both laughed nervously. They never thought their body language gave away that much.

"I'm glad you asked," Yared said. And he explained what happened. "We had our first kiss at Yeha. And that historical place became a landmark in our love life."

After Yared's remark, both Tsehay and Yared looked like they were about to go fifteen years back in their memory.

Before he lost them, Ezana reminded them of his other question about what happened at Abba Garima Monastery.

"That's my favorite," Tsehay said. "After our first kiss at Yeha, we went straight to Abba Garima. The priest, who was our tour guide in the monastery, showered us with blessings. And we both startled when he said, 'God bless your marriage.' I believed it was a clear sign from God."

Once the gate to their love story opened, Ezana took advantage of it and asked them more questions. They narrated their love journey that took fifteen years. When they disagreed on some accounts, Ezana asked them to answer with their versions.

"Guess what? It's a beautiful story, and I accepted it as my birthday gift. Thank you, and I love you both." Ezana kissed them.

***

Ashenda, the most colorful girls' festival celebrated annually in Mekelle, Tigray became a perfect climax for the family to end their incredible vacation.

The girls' beauty, their costume, hairdo, and jewelry, the mesmerizing music, and the dancing combined made the festivity out of this world.

Yared and Ezana barely saw Tsehay for three days. Females were supposed to be free during the Ashenda celebration, and they let her have the time of her life.

"I must agree with Mom. This is the most awesome women's festival on the planet," Ezana said after observing the entire female nation come out glamorously to celebrate the event.

73

EZANA BACK IN SCHOOL

B ack in Denver, Colorado, unlike his past school years, Ezana felt excited to go back to school. The anxiety, the fear, and the sleepless nights were gone. Instead, he couldn't wait to go back to school and tell his miraculous experience to his classmates. His view of the world was changed, and he became even more faithful to God than ever before. The trip and the extraordinary experience with the lovebird made him humble. He felt he was a boy with a sense of purpose in life.

He called some of his close friends, including his dearest, Grace. He was so thrilled that he was about to tell her what happened in Aksum. Fortunately, she had to go somewhere with her mom and had to hang up the phone before he opened up. Most of the friends he called thought he sounded weird. Only Grace felt the transformation, and she knew he had a story to tell.

***

B oys and girls, let's make our first day of school fun. How did you spend your summer? Who wants to go first?" the teacher asked. Grace raised her hand quickly. The teacher gave her the chance to go first.

"I think Ezana has a story to tell," she said.

The class was amazed that Ezana even came to school on the first day, and Grace took everyone by surprise when she nominated him to go first. Most of the students laughed and dared both Grace and Ezana.

"Ezana, is that true?" the teacher asked. All eyes stared at Ezana.

Opposite to their expectation, Ezana was ready to go.

"Yes, sir." Ezana strode from the back of the class to the front.

The students' eyes panned with him. The teacher left the stage for Ezana and sat on his chair. Grace crossed her fingers.

Ezana appeared different. He was confident and relaxed, more as a teacher than as a student. The way he carried himself on the stage got him the undivided attention of the class. Even the boys who tried to undermine him shut their mouths.

Ezana was dying to tell his story and didn't waste time to start narrating it. He knew the kind of story his classmates liked to hear, and he jumped straight into his magical adventures with the lovebird.

However, the interest of the class to listen to him fell instantly. None of them could buy his miraculous story. Some of the students booed him. Others started snoring. A couple of bad boys threw paper balls in his face. The teacher begged and yelled to ease the class.

Ezana didn't expect it. His smile faded, his confidence started leaving his body, and his legs began shaking. He wanted to leave the room but wasn't sure if his legs could carry him out.

Suddenly, he felt something on his shoulder, and he saw students ducking under their desks, jumping out of the window, and running around scared and clueless.

"Bird?" Ezana breathed, and his whole body electrified in a thrill.

"I got your back, buddy!" the lovebird said proudly.

"But it's eight thousand miles. How did you—"

"Did you get the chance to read Matthew 19:26?" the lovebird asked.

"Jesus looked at them and said, 'With man, this is impossible, but with God, all things are possible,'" Ezana said.

"Right. With God, all things are possible," the lovebird emphasized.

Ezana realized he was invisible, and that was the reason his classmates were terrorized. He saw Grace sat quietly, believing and expecting a miracle. Others who couldn't escape through the door or the window were scared. The teacher remained still in the corner, terrified.

The lovebird jumped off his shoulder to let him become visible. *Boom!* He appeared.

Some of the remaining students flew out of the window, screaming.

***

What happened in the seventh-grade class spread in the school and to the neighbors as fast as the speed of light. Everyone wanted to hear Ezana's awesome adventures with the lovebird, and all the cool boys and girls became his friends. Since that day, Ezana became a legend.

74

THE CALL TO ADVENTURE

Ezana stumbled on something in his room. He pulled it out from under his clothes.

"How did I forget to unwrap and hang it on my wall?"

He unwrapped the gift his grandparents presented him in Aksum. He couldn't believe his eyes. He blinked twice.

He read the title of the painting: "Chapel of the Tablet." His jaw dropped in surprise.

ACKNOWLEDGEMENTS

M any people have played significant roles in inspiring me to write this book. Several helped and encouraged me during the process of writing.

Multiple families and friends took their time and went the extra mile to read and improve the manuscript. I am forever grateful to all.

Special thanks to Solomon Mengesha, Dr. Desta Haileselassie, FitsumBerhan Teka, Girmay Hagos, Betanya M. Tefera, Daniel Tsegay, Wainnie Tewelde, Yohannes Gigar, Mikail N. Zekiros, Genet Kassa and Family, Esrom & Efrata Kibrom, Gebremariam Hailu, Eyerusalem Berhane and my editor Meagan. Thank you all so much.